ASHES TO ASHES

An Allison Parker Mystery

Adair Sanders

ISBN: 1539835731
ISBN 13: 9781539835738

TO MY READERS

As with the other Allison Parker mysteries, this third book in the series is a complete work of fiction. While I draw on personal knowledge and may use the names of actual locales and businesses, the story itself is the one created solely by the characters as they appear to me when I sit in front of my computer.

Enjoy.

IN THE BEGINNING...

"Nine-one-one. What is your emergency?" The operator's voice barely permeated the fog that encased his mind like a shroud. "Hello?" the woman's voice inquired a second time. "Nine-one-one. What is your emergency?"

A groan slid from Frank's lips as he struggled to make a response. "Shot," he whispered. "Bad."

"Sir, can you give me your location?" the operator asked, at the same time initiating the emergency system's phone-tracking software.

"Old Anderson homeplace...Route 14." An involuntary shudder racked Frank's body, increasing the flow of hot, sticky liquid he could feel spilling from his gut. "Not...who I...thought..."

"Stay with me, sir," the operator's voice demanded. "Help is on the way."

"Too…late." Bloody fingers released their grip on the black cell phone. *What a shitty way to die,* Frank thought as the last wisps of consciousness abandoned him to the grave.

CHAPTER ONE

"Jim, don't forget we've got Megan and Tim's wedding Saturday," Allison called to her husband. "Donna offered to stay the weekend with Charlotte and Mack, so I found a B and B near Eufala. We won't have to come back till Sunday."

Wiping remnants of Gillette's best from his handsome face, Judge Jim Kaufman peered inside his wife's walk-in closet and replied, "It's been on my calendar since we got the invitation. I've cleared my docket for Friday afternoon. If the weather's good, I thought we'd put the top down on your new ride and take the backroads."

"Perfect," Allison replied before turning her attention to several suits hanging in front of her. Pulling a muted plaid from its neighbors, Allison mused aloud, "Maybe this one for the hearing today?"

"What case is it?" Jim asked, buttoning up the white oxford he always wore under his black judicial robes.

"A motion hearing in the Craddock discrimination case. The arbitrator is driving over from Birmingham. Jack Striker's representing the defendant." A thoughtful smile tickled the corners of Allison's mouth as she reflected on how the previous year's Boudreaux case had changed the nature of her law practice. Although one of her firm's clients had tried to kill her, the settlement her partner, David Jackson, had obtained for the would-be murderer in a totally unrelated civil case had enabled Parker & Jackson to begin accepting pro bono cases without worrying about how the firm's overhead and staff would be paid.

The Craddock matter was a case in point. Young, poor, and pregnant, Juanita Craddock had been fired from her job as a waitress at the Kickoff, a popular Fort Charles sports bar and restaurant, once her condition had become apparent. Before long, the few dollars Juanita had managed to put back for an emergency were nearly depleted. Forced to choose between eating and paying her rent, Juanita had packed a small suitcase with her few meager belongings and moved to the Salvation Army's homeless shelter.

Stepping into a pair of gray pumps, Allison checked her appearance in the bedroom's full-length mirror. Today's hearing was an important one for her client, and Allison planned to convey a position of strength with her appearance as well as with her legal arguments. "Thank goodness Donna's sister volunteers at the shelter," Allison remarked to Jim, "and found out about what happened to Juanita." Shaking her head, Allison continued. "I'm amazed that after all these years, companies still think they can discriminate against pregnant women."

It was Jim's turn to smile. "And I'm certain you are going to teach them the error of their ways," he observed, giving his wife a quick kiss on his way out of the bedroom. "You can tell me all about it tonight. And now," he said, checking his watch, "I've got to get Charlotte and Mack to school."

How lucky am I? Allison asked herself a few minutes later, watching her husband's SUV exit the long driveway leading from their farmhouse to the road. *A husband who runs carpool.* Picking up her briefcase from the kitchen table where she had left it the night before, Allison stopped to pour a second cup of the day's coffee into a go-cup and headed for her car.

The twenty-minute drive to downtown Fort Charles would allow Allison just enough time for one last mental run-through on the testimony and evidence she intended to present in the Craddock matter later that morning.

The law offices of Parker & Jackson occupied half of an older, two-story commercial building located a few blocks from the town center. Surrounded by newer and shinier buildings, the seeming interloper had impressed Allison with its comfy aura the first time she saw the structure. A low-slung shingled roof reached out over second-floor casement windows, endowing the smallish structure with a welcoming facade. A pair of large bay windows adorned the front of the main floor, two old oak doors indicating office space for more than one tenant. As luck would have it, the owner of the building and its only occupant was Frank Martin, a private investigator who had been instrumental in helping Allison solve her first mystery. Two years ago, upon hearing that Allison was starting her own firm, Frank had offered Parker & Jackson the other half of the building at a favorable rental rate. The unofficial partnership between the law firm and the private investigator had spawned both friendship and business.

As Allison made the turn from Main Street to Fourth Avenue, the sight of two county squad cars, lights flashing, parked in front of Parker & Jackson drove all thoughts of the Craddock case from her mind. Several uniformed officers stood on the narrow sidewalk, one of whom appeared to be interrogating Allison's secretary, Donna Pevey. *What is Donna doing on the sidewalk?* Allison couldn't imagine what could be going on. *Where is David? Or Frank?* Quickly pulling her Miata into its designated space, Allison bolted from the car and ran toward the crowd that had gathered in the front of the building.

"Rob!" Allison called, recognizing one of Sheriff Trowbridge's young deputies. "What's going on?" she demanded as she closed the distance between them. "Stop talking," Allison ordered as she passed her secretary, "at least until I find out what all of this is about."

Deputy Robinson leaned close to Allison's ear and whispered, "Ms. Parker, Sheriff Trowbridge is inside Martin Investigations. He said to send you in as soon as you arrived."

Allison ignored the deputy's directive. "Why is my secretary being interrogated on the street?"

"I'm not being interrogated, Allison." Donna hurried to assure her boss. "You really need to talk to the sheriff." The serious tone, accompanied by the look on her secretary's face caused a shiver to run up Allison's spine.

"Is it—" A terrible thought gripped Allison.

"Oh, no, no. It's not the judge or your children." Donna grabbed Allison's hand. "It's Frank."

The sight that greeted Allison inside the front door of Martin Investigations failed to offer her any reassurance about the gravity of whatever it was that was going on. Sheila McMurray, Frank's new secretary, was sobbing on Sheriff Trowbridge's shoulder, causing a large wet spot on the sheriff's otherwise starched and pristine uniform.

"Toby, what's happened? Where's Frank?" Allison touched the sheriff's arm to get his attention. "Why are all these deputies outside?"

Ignoring Allison, the sheriff gently led the distraught secretary to a nearby chair in the office's reception area. "Ms. McMurray, I'll have one of my deputies drive you home. My office will keep you informed of Mr. Martin's condition."

Allison didn't like the word *condition*, but she knew it meant Frank was still alive. For how long, or how bad he was, she intended to find out. "Toby," Allison's tone demanded the sheriff's attention, "Donna said you wanted to see me. What has happened to Frank? Where is he?"

"Nine-one-one got a call today around three forty-five a.m. The caller said he'd been shot, and it was bad." Toby stopped, grimaced, and continued. "No one knew it was Frank until the EMTs and one of my deputies arrived."

"But he's alive, right?" Allison interrupted.

"Yes"—the sheriff nodded—"but just barely. He lost a lot of blood, and he's had a good bit of internal damage. Nasty gut shots tend to have that effect on the victim."

"Where is he?"

"The ER doc at Fort Charles General stabilized him, then decided to airlift him to Birmingham. It's going to be touch and go for the next forty-eight hours. Frank's surgery options are better at the med center," the sheriff explained.

Allison nodded grimly. "What can I do, Toby? Is there a reason you asked for me?"

"I know you and Frank sometimes consult on crossover matters," the sheriff replied. "I was hoping you would know why Frank was out at the old Anderson homeplace in the middle of the night."

"I have no idea." Allison shrugged. "Frank and I haven't worked a case together in several months. I had no idea he was onto something dangerous."

"His secretary hasn't been of much use either," Toby added. "Sheila said she's been working for Frank for only three weeks. She hadn't even learned who his current clients might be."

"Well, she better be quicker on the uptake than that," Allison observed, "or she won't be working for Frank for very much longer." Turning to leave, Allison hoped her last words weren't prophetic more for Frank's sake than for Sheila McMurray's. Frank was family, and Allison wasn't ready to let him go.

CHAPTER TWO

A level-one trauma center, the University of Alabama Hospital was recognized as one of the twenty largest and best-equipped hospitals in the country. Boasting more than 1,150 beds, UAB combined its role as a teaching hospital with world-class medical research to provide patients with the most innovative and up-to-date treatments available. UAB's Emergency Department furthered that reputation. With round-the-clock access to top-notch specialists, UAB's ED was the go-to choice for critically injured patients like Frank Martin. Had Frank been conscious, he would have been both thankful and worried to find himself admitted to that facility.

It had taken some convincing before the critical care unit charge nurse would allow Allison and Jim into Frank's cubicle. When a series of polite requests failed to persuade the guardian of the CCU to allow them entry, Jim had pulled the judge card. In short order, Allison and Jim found themselves by Frank's bed, disbelieving the sight that lay before them on the narrow, white-sheeted bed.

"Oh my God," Allison whispered to her husband. "He looks like death."

Frank's usually ruddy complexion was a close match to the sheets on which he lay. Two IV poles holding bags of unknown fluids stood at the head of the hospital bed, the lines leading from the suspended bags snaking their way into small entry ports on both of Frank's arms. Most alarming to Allison was the intubation tube protruding from Frank's mouth.

"He's worse than I thought," she admitted.

Jim wrapped his arm around his wife. "Frank's a fighter, Allison. I know he looks bad, but you can't count him out yet. Let's see what the doctor has to say."

Tears began to roll down Allison's face. Gently, she stroked Frank's pale hand, then softly squeezed his fingers. "Don't you die on me, Frank." She sniffed. "I mean it. Don't you dare die on me."

What are you talking about woman? Frank shouted at Allison. Why wasn't she paying attention to what he was trying to tell her? *What are you and the judge doing here? Why are you talking to that fat guy on the bed?* What was all of this sadness about? He was just fine—except that for some reason he seemed to be floating up near the ceiling of this strange room. *Judge,* Frank demanded, *up here. I'm up here.* Why couldn't the judge and Allison see him? None of this made any sense.

"Judge Kaufman, Ms. Parker, I'm Dr. Lopez," a woman obviously too young to have attended medical school addressed Jim and Allison. "The charge nurse paged me about your arrival."

Jim extended his hand, acknowledging the doctor's reprimand. "Allison and I appreciate the exception to scheduled visiting hours. We drove up from Fort Charles as soon as we could after Sheriff Trowbridge notified us about what had happened. Frank doesn't have any blood family, but he's as much a part of our family as is humanly possible."

Getting no response from the doctor, Allison interjected what she hoped would be received as a further apology. "My husband was a patient here last year after a gunshot wound. We know Frank is receiving excellent care."

"Does getting shot run in your family?" Dr. Lopez inquired dryly.

"Not generally," Jim replied. "I was shot in the midst of an FBI sting operation. We don't know how Frank got shot, or who shot him."

So much for trying to be nice, Allison thought. "My husband was shot saving my life. Frank was likely shot tracking a criminal. How either of them was shot is irrelevant, *Doctor*." Allison fought to control what she really wanted to say to this teenager masquerading in a physician's coat. "What *is* relevant is Frank's prognosis and treatment."

The sheepish look on Dr. Lopez's face acknowledged receipt of Allison's intended message. "You're right, Ms. Parker. All that matters is Mr. Martin's care and prognosis." Flipping several pages on Frank's medical chart, the young doctor gathered her composure and continued. "The doctors in Fort Charles did a good job stabilizing Mr. Martin before he was transported to us. His surgery here early this morning was successful. We've placed Mr. Martin in a coma and intubated him to allow his body to rest and to promote a more rapid healing." Putting aside the chart, Dr. Lopez hesitated. "There was some internal damage. We had to remove Mr. Martin's spleen and a portion of his stomach."

The shushing of the ventilator intruded on the room's silence as Allison digested the unsavory news. "I know the spleen isn't necessary." Allison's response was subdued. "How much intestine did you take? What is the long-term effect of that action?"

"It's true you can live without a spleen," Dr. Lopez replied, "but because that organ plays such a crucial role in the body's ability to fight off bacteria, Mr. Martin will be more susceptible to infections such as pneumonia and some forms of meningitis. We'll be giving him vaccinations to cover these bacteria before he is released from the hospital."

"And his stomach?" Jim prompted.

"Fortunately, we had to remove only a portion of the small intestine. Most people who have this surgery recover fully and are able to resume the same activities they were doing before their surgery." Dr. Lopez smiled. "Mr. Martin's biggest obstacle to recovery will be his excessive weight. He needs to lose at least fifty pounds."

Good luck with that, Allison thought. "When do you plan to bring Frank out of the coma?"

"We'll let him rest a few more days. He had significant blood loss, and while the long-term effect won't be noticeable, that coupled with the surgery has caused Mr. Martin's body a significant trauma. If you've no other questions"—the doctor gave Allison and Jim a stern look—"visiting hours are over."

Frank watched as the judge and Allison followed the doctor from the room. He still couldn't figure out who the fat guy was in the bed with all those machines hooked up to him. That girl in the white coat seemed to think the fat guy was him, but Frank knew that couldn't be right. And why did Allison and Jim look so worried? Did they know the fat guy? Well, it wasn't his problem. Frank felt relaxed and happy. Maybe he'd just hang out here for a while longer.

CHAPTER THREE

The sky above the Calhoun County Sheriff's Office had that greenish-gray look that often preceded really bad weather. Toby wondered if he should make a quick call to his contact at the National Weather Service in Birmingham to see if trouble was headed toward his county. *Better safe than sorry*, he thought, punching in the ten-digit number that would connect him to the NWS's regional office. Tornadoes were a way of life in Dixie Alley, the area across the Deep South known for the numerous violent spring and fall storms that had a habit of creating havoc and causing damage. Calhoun County, Alabama, had been fortunate over the years. Only one death had ever been attributed to a tornado, and that one had—in the sheriff's mind—been a blessing in disguise for the victim. Finding what was left of the New Orleans prostitute after the tornado last year had taken most of her had started Toby, and eventually the FBI, on a multistate search for a serial killer. Reflecting on the outcome of that case, Toby hoped to one day receive a call informing him that the killer had been shived in prison.

After a brief conversation with his contact at the weather service who assured him that today's sky was no harbinger of disaster, Sheriff Trowbridge turned his attention to the mess of paper scattered across his desk. Sheila McMurray had delivered all of her new boss's open case files to Toby the day before. There weren't that many; over the years, Frank Martin had become adept at not taking on more than his one-man show could handle.

"There's just five open cases that I could find," Sheila apologized as she handed over the short stack of manila folders. "Two surveillance cases involving married couples, one background investigation for Sheriff Gilbert over in Meridian, one that has something to do with an inheritance, and this last one"— Sheila had handed over a thin file that appeared empty—"just a name. Nothing much, but I figured you'd want to see it just in case."

The two surveillance cases involved spying on an alleged unfaithful spouse. Frank had mentioned to Toby more than once that taking what he called cheater cases were the bread and butter of private investigator work that paid the bills. Toby smiled remembering Frank's comment. "When people start thinking with their dick or pussy, there's no telling what crazy shit they'll do. Never in a million years do they think they'll get caught."

Opening the manila folder marked "Goodpasture," Toby figured Frank's client had to be Evelyn, the wife. Her husband, Miles, was thought by many in certain Fort Charles circles to have more than a wandering eye. *Who'd have thought?* Toby whispered when he saw the pictures of Evelyn in flagrante delicto with a man Toby had never seen. Clearly, there was a side to Evelyn Goodpasture that the upright citizens of his county had not suspicioned. Maybe Evelyn had decided to get even with her philandering husband. Whatever the reason, Toby knew who was going to get the short end of the stick if Miles Goodpasture filed for divorce. There was a big difference between gossip and black-and-white photos.

Setting aside the evidence of Evelyn Goodpasture's romp, Toby picked up the second cheater file. The name on the file, Marshall Randall, drew a blank for Toby. Fort Charles and Calhoun County had a small-enough population that the sheriff had either a personal acquaintance with or passing knowledge of just about every family living in his jurisdiction. Toby was fairly certain he'd never heard of a Randall family. Opening the folder, Toby was surprised to find it practically empty. A client intake sheet was clipped to the inside of the file, and a short note in what looked like Frank's writing was clipped on the opposite side. The dearth of information was explained by the date on the client intake form. Frank had just been hired by Marshall Randall a week earlier. Plus, Randall was from Montgomery. Frank's notes indicated his client had not wanted to hire anyone in his own town to follow his wife. *Makes sense,* Toby thought. *An incognito PI.*

Cheater cases could be nasty, no doubt about it. Toby knew that from experience and having been called to more than one domestic violence fight. Miles Goodpasture might divorce Evelyn after he took a look at Frank's work product, but Toby didn't see Evelyn Goodpasture trying to kill Frank as a result of being caught. Frank hadn't had enough time to do much on the Randall case, so Toby dismissed Marshall Randall and his wife as potential murderers—Frank hadn't had time to piss off either the client or the target.

The case for Sheriff Scott Gilbert, Toby's counterpart in Meridian, Mississippi, might have more potential. Gilbert had retained Frank to take a look at the extracurricular activities of Melvin and Rocky Shipley. The Shipley boys, known around Toby's office as the Shitly brothers were local lowlifes, in and out of trouble with the law, mainly for misdemeanors, bar brawls, and public drunkenness charges. One of Sheriff Gilbert's snitches had tagged Melvin and Rocky as the recipients of flat-screen TVs that had been stolen from the Meridian Walmart. Frank had been hired to pose, while wearing a wire, as a potential buyer of the hot merchandise. According to Frank's case file, the sting was to occur next Wednesday. The Shipley brothers might be stupid, but they weren't dumb enough to try to kill someone even if they had somehow caught wind of the upcoming sting. Toby made a note to call Sheriff Gilbert. Scott would have to find someone else to wear the wire.

Having discarded three of the five case files as not producing a lead as to Frank's attacker, Toby turned his attention to the file Sheila had identified as having to do with an inheritance. A quick glance at the file's contents moved this fourth file to the reject pile. Frank had been hired to track down Elizabeth Rader's niece and nephew by the executor of Elizabeth's estate. Residing in New Mexico and Oregon, respectively, Bitsy Rader Ragsdale and Philip Rader were the only heirs to their spinster aunt's house, bank account, and a few stocks—simple, straightforward, and no other heirs bitching about the bequests. The Rader file was another dead end.

The last file was a mystery. The intake sheet gave scant information. A name, a phone number with a Florida area code and a picture of a horse. No address. No notes. When Frank had opened this file was another mystery. The intake sheet was undated and unsigned by anyone including Frank. *Odd*, thought Toby. The intake sheets on the other four files had been signed by the client and initialed by Frank. *Well, there's only one thing to do*, Toby reasoned. Dialing the Florida number, Toby wondered who would answer.

"McIntosh Farms," a voice with a hint of a Scottish brogue flowed pleasantly into Toby's ear.

"This is Calhoun County, Alabama, Sheriff Toby Trowbridge. I'm trying to track down the person who hired Martin Investigations in Fort Charles, Alabama." Toby introduced himself, hoping his formal title would generate more answers than questions from the man at the other end of the line.

"Is that so?" came a doubtful reply. "And how might I be knowing ye're tellin' me the truth?"

"Do you know Frank Martin?" Toby decided to change tactics.

"I might," the man allowed. "What does he look like?"

Toby debated whether to give Frank's description. The guy at McIntosh Farms, whatever that was, seemed awfully wary. Maybe there was more to this case file than the slim contents implied. Figuring the pros outweighed the cons, Toby replied, "Big guy, about six two, three hundred and twenty pounds give or take, doesn't tolerate crap"—Toby paused— "or jack around his sheriff with nonsense." *Like you're doing right now,* Toby added his last comment silently.

A loud guffaw erupted into Toby's ear. "Yep, that'd be Frankie boy. And I know who ye are, too, Mr. Sheriff. Frankie told me all about you."

What the heck? Toby asked himself. The sheriff was pretty certain he'd never heard of McIntosh Farms, and he sure as hell had never heard anyone call Frank Martin "Frankie." "Please identify yourself," Toby ordered. "Who are you, how long have you known Frank Martin, and are you the person who recently retained Mr. Martin to conduct an investigation?"

"Calm yerself, Sheriff. I've been knowing Frankie since we was wee lads. Just lost track over the years. Didn't even know he was right up the road, so to speak, until I read about that serial killer he helped catch last year." Toby heard a door close at the other end of the line before the man continued. "Me name's Sean McIntosh. I'm Frankie's fourth cousin on his mam's side."

"I've known Frank Martin for almost twenty years. I've never heard him mention you," Toby replied. "In fact, Frank told me he had no family. Parents dead, no brothers or sisters, no mention of cousins close or distant."

"That's no surprise," Sean McIntosh offered. "We hadn't seen each other since we were seven or eight. That's when my mother married Patrick McIntosh, and we moved to Scotland. My stepdad adopted me. I didn't return to the States until a few years ago when I decided to expand McIntosh Farms. Florida's a good place for raising thorough-breds."

"Why did you contact Frank?" Toby asked. "For a family reunion or to hire him?"

"Both, actually. Like I told ye, I didn't know where Frankie was until I saw that article last year about the serial killer. I should have called him then, but you know how it is starting up a new business, I just let it slide." Toby listened while McIntosh proffered an explanation. "But when Scarlet disappeared and the authorities down here reached a dead end, I thought of Frankie."

"So you hired Frank to find a missing person?"

"Not a person," McIntosh replied with a huff. "Blue Scarlet is a horse—an expensive, thorough-bred horse insured for four mil."

This case is getting crazier by the minute. No wonder there isn't much in Frank's case file.

"Mr. McIntosh, did you report the theft of your horse?"

"I most certainly did," came an indignant reply. "Do ye take me for an idiot? I don't want the money. I want me horse."

"Has your insurance company completed its investigation?" Toby was afraid to hear the answer.

"Yes."

"And?" Toby prompted.

"They told me there was no record of Blue Scarlet."

"Excuse me?" Toby was confused. "What do you mean there was no record?"

"Are ye daft?" McIntosh growled. "The pinheads at the insurance company told me there was no Blue Scarlet, that no horse had been registered by that name, that I'd never insured her. They actually suggested I see a psychiatrist!"

Maybe they were onto something, Toby considered. Sean McIntosh sounded like he had a screw loose, for sure. "I hate to be the one to bring this news to you," Toby began, changing the subject. "Frank was shot two days ago. He's alive but in CCU at the university hospital in Birmingham. Obviously, he won't be able to do any work for a while. You'll want to hire someone else to help you locate your horse."

A sharp, hissing intake of breath slipped from the phone. "They'll be after me next," Sean McIntosh whispered.

The buzz of a disconnected line replaced Sean McIntosh's gentle brogue. Pondering the strange conversation and its abrupt ending, Toby reached for the cup of coffee that had most certainly turned cold during his phone call with McIntosh. What had Frank gotten involved in? Was the scenario that he had just heard simply the disturbed hallucinations of some old man? Toby wasn't convinced that this Sean McIntosh was Frank's long-lost cousin, but he knew truth when he heard it, and it was clear to Toby that McIntosh knew what Frank looked like. Hell, Frank had an open file on McIntosh Farms. But was the investigation one initiated by McIntosh, or was McIntosh Farms the target of the investigation initiated by a third party? Draining the last sips of cold caffeine, Toby remembered Frank's words to the 911 operator: "Not...who I...thought."

CHAPTER FOUR

I t had been over a week since Frank Martin had been shot and almost killed. Kicking black, patent leather high heels from her weary feet, Allison tossed her briefcase on the sofa in her office and slid her tired self into the oversized, leather cocoon on wheels that passed as her desk chair. Allison hadn't heard a peep from the sheriff since she talked to him the day Frank had been shot. She couldn't decide if this was good news or bad. Allison and Frank had worked a couple of cases for Sheriff Trowbridge over the past two years, but Allison had a feeling that the sheriff had never really been comfortable with his civilian helpers. Still, he had sought her out that other morning, hoping that she might have a lead on who Frank had been meeting at the Anderson place. She hadn't.

Other than the brief time Allison and her husband had carved out to make the run to UAB to check on Frank, Allison had been too swamped with work and hearings for her own clients to turn her attention to matters Frank might have been investigating, or to get back to Birmingham for another visit to Frank's bedside. *At least he's not getting any worse,* Allison reflected. True to her word, the young doctor tending to Frank had provided Allison and Jim a daily update on Frank's condition once they had provided her with the medical power of attorney Frank had made the year before appointing Allison and Jim as his agents. Noticing the blinking red light on her desk phone, Allison punched the Replay button. Hopefully, this would be Dr. Lopez with a better report than yesterday.

"Ms. Parker, this is Dr. Lopez. I would prefer to speak with you in person about this development, but your secretary said she wasn't sure when you would be out of court. I won't be available to talk later today, and I wanted to make sure you got this information before tomorrow." Allison didn't like how this message was starting off. Taking the phone off speaker mode, Allison pulled the receiver to her ear. "We reduced the medicine we had been giving

Mr. Martin to keep him in a medically induced coma," Dr. Lopez's message continued. "Although his injuries are certainly showing signs of healing, Mr. Martin has not regained consciousness. At this point, we are not overly worried. Some patients take longer than others to recover from the effects of a medically induced coma. It is more likely than not that this is the case with Mr. Martin. However, if Mr. Martin's condition has not improved within twenty-four hours, we will need to consult further with you and your husband."

Allison slowly replaced the phone in its cradle. Part of her was not surprised by the doctor's message. Despite what Dr. Lopez had assured Allison earlier in the week, Allison had harbored a fear that Frank was much worse than the doctor was telling her. The Frank Martin she knew was strong, a bear of a man, loud and overbearing with those he didn't know well but kind, considerate, and loyal to those he loved—and there were many more people in the latter category than most would think. The man she had seen in the bed in the CCU had none of Frank's vitality. Yes, she told herself, he was unconscious, but even so, Allison believed there would have been a palpable sense of Frank's energy in the quiet hospital cubicle.

Frank was in good hands, medically speaking. Of this Allison had no doubt. There was nothing she could do for him that the doctors at UAB couldn't do five thousand times better. What she could do, Allison considered, was find out who had done this to Frank. Feeling the fatigue fall from her shoulders, Allison dialed Sheriff Trowbridge's private line.

"Allison," the sheriff answered, caller ID announcing Allison before she could say a word.

"Toby," Allison replied. This was a call for a personal favor. Using the sheriff's title might make denying her request easier for the county's chief law enforcement officer. Allison intended to use all she had to her advantage. "I just got a call from Dr. Lopez. It's not good news."

"Is he alive?" the sheriff blurted.

"Yes, for now," Allison's reply was soft and low. "He hasn't come out of the coma the doctors put him in after his surgery. Dr. Lopez is giving him another twenty-four hours before considering what to do next."

"Shit!" Toby cursed. "Shit and shit again!" Then, remembering he was talking to a judge's wife, he added, "Sorry, Allison."

"You don't need to be sorry about anything other than Frank's current condition," Allison assured the sheriff. "You've simply expressed the same sentiments I had listening to Dr. Lopez's message."

"What else did Dr. Lopez say?"

"That's about it. She left a message because I was in court and she was going to be unavailable later," Allison explained. "I think the real test will be whether Frank regains consciousness in the next twenty-four hours. Dr. Lopez seemed cautiously optimistic about that—or at least that's the impression I got from the tone she used."

"Well, thanks for the call. Let me know what you hear tomorrow."

Allison heard the good-bye in Toby's reply and interrupted. "That's not the only reason I was calling. I want in."

"You want in what?" Toby asked. "Wait a minute. You mean you want in on the investigation of who nearly killed Frank? Is that what you're asking?" He knew it was. "No way, Allison."

"Toby Trowbridge, you listen to me. Frank Martin is family. I'm not about to sit on the sidelines on this." Allison's raised voice indicated her rising temper. "His quick thinking last year saved my life. I owe him." *And I'd do this even if I didn't owe him a life debt.*

Several scenarios ran concurrently through Toby's head. Most of them ended with Judge Kaufman handing Toby his walking papers for letting his wife get involved in another dangerous adventure. Toby knew the judge didn't have any control over hiring or firing the sheriff, but he wasn't so sure about what the judge might do otherwise if Toby allowed Allison to get hurt. Whatever happened, the judge would be sure to think it was Toby's fault. He's seen Judge Kaufman in action when Allison's life had been threatened. Toby had no intention of being the target of that kind of controlled anger and vengeance.

"I cannot allow you in the field again," Toby replied in his best authoritarian voice. Sensing a quick objection from Allison, the sheriff rapidly continued. "But I do need some help doing some background research on one of Frank's current cases." Toby outlined his conversation with Sean McIntosh, adding his suspicions about McIntosh's alleged relationship to Frank. "I don't have anyone in the department right now that I can spare for research on something that is probably nothing. You can help Frank, and help me, by taking a hard look at Sean McIntosh, at McIntosh Farms, and particularly his claim about being Frank's cousin. Of all the cases Frank was working on, this one has the most potential."

Allison fumed. Taking no for an answer didn't sit well with her one little bit. But this was only a partial no. *One step at a time*, she reminded herself. "Well"— she sighed, hoping she was conveying the appropriate amount of acquiescence—"it's better than doing nothing. Have Beth send over photocopies of what you've got on McIntosh, or better yet, just e-mail me a copy of your notes from your conversation with the guy. I'll see what I can find out."

"Thanks, Allison." The Sheriff sounded relieved. "This will be a big help, and no telling what you'll be able to uncover."

Damn straight. And if I find something, you won't be the first to know. Allison smiled at the thought. Two could play this game.

CHAPTER FIVE

Four Years Ago

B ell, Florida, was a sad little town. Situated in the northern and central part of the state, the town had been founded in the 1890s and named after a beauty contest winner long since forgotten. Comprised of less than two square miles and fewer than five hundred residents, the most that could be said for Bell was that Gainesville was only thirty minutes away. Contrary to what one would expect from a sleepy, hole-in-the-road kind of town, Bell had the misfortune of being the place where, in 2014, Don Charles Spirit had murdered his daughter and her six children before turning the gun on himself.

Bell police officers were horrified by the carnage—nothing like that had ever happened in Bell—and more than one officer afterward reconsidered his or her line of work.

Predominately white—to the tune of more than 95 percent of the population—Bell was also a poor town. Median income for a family barely cleared thirty grand a year, while single males earned almost ten thousand a year less than that. Devoid of industry or significant job opportunity, it was no surprise that almost 20 percent of the residents in Bell lived below the poverty level. Most of the available work, and only to those with transportation of some reliable sort, was found at the farms and ranches in surrounding areas. Living on minimum wage was hard, but it was better than starving.

Jorge Velasquez tilted the metal canteen, sucking in the last drop of moisture from the uncapped vessel, and considered his options. He'd done seasonal work, but he didn't much like it. Sure, it was an honest way to earn money, but sleeping accommodations for the workers weren't generally much better than what one would find for a farm animal. Jorge might be poor, but that didn't give anyone the right to expect him to live like a pig. The woman at the bodega outside Gainesville hadn't been much help either. All she'd known about were a couple of farms near Bell, which she described as a hick gringo town a few miles away where people like him weren't welcome. Jorge had just about convinced himself that one more stint picking strawberries was better than no job at all, no matter how hostile the natives, when his eyes had settled on a small advertisement pinned to the job board near the bodega's checkout counter. *Horse groom needed. $600/wk, room provided, McIntosh Farms.* A number and name were listed in smaller print.

Twisting the cap on the now-empty canteen, Jorge reached a decision. Ambling back to the bodega, the immigrant plunked several quarters on the wooden counter loudly enough to get the attention of the shopkeeper he had spoken with earlier. "This enough for a local call?"

"*Si*," the woman replied, quickly counting the money. "Ten minutes. No more," she added, pulling a small cell phone from her skirt pocket.

Jorge dialed the number on the advertisement. Five desolate rings echoed in his ear before, at last, a voice answered. "McIntosh Farms."

"Uh, I'm calling about the groomer job. That still available?" Jorge held the small phone between his shoulder and jaw while he scrounged his pockets for a tattered pack of Marlboros.

"Matter of fact, it is, laddie." The Scottish accent surprised Jorge. Maybe he'd have a chance at the job after all. The guy at the other end of the phone

34

clearly wasn't a local. "What experience might you have with the horses?"

Jorge wrestled with the truth. He's been raised around horses in Guatemala, but that was a long time ago. He could ride, any fool could rub down a horse, and with a little practice he'd pick back up any other skills that might be required. "Senor, I was raised with many horses. I will do a good job for you." Jorge waited to see if he'd have to actually lie.

"We'll see about that," the Scotsman replied. "If you don't, you'll be out on your spic ass before the sun goes down."

Anger boiled up in Jorge's throat. *Fucking bigot, gringo.* He didn't need a job that badly. An instant before Jorge started to tell his prospective employer to perform an unnatural act, a burst of laughter interceded.

"Good for you," the Scotsman praised Jorge. "Glad to see you can hold your temper. You'll need to in this godforsaken backwater. You'll be called that and worse every time you go to town for me. You still want this job?" he asked.

Pulling the last cigarette from the crumpled pack, and counting the seven dollars he had left, Jorge decided name calling couldn't hurt him. "*Sí,* senor. I do. When can I start?"

"As soon as you can. Where are you calling me from?"

"The bodega on County Road 342, 'bout five miles outside Bell."

"I know it. Be there in forty, give or take," the Scotsman replied. "Unless you got your own transportation, which I doubt." Before Jorge could answer, the man continued. "Of course you don't. You wouldn't be looking for this kind of work if you had any other option."

While he waited for his new employer, Jorge wondered if he had made a mistake. There wasn't anything wrong with being a groomer. Why would the man have made the comment about other options? Maybe he should have asked the woman in the bodega if she knew anything about some Scotsman living in the area. Brushing the dust from the seat of his pants, Jorge hauled his body off the curb and ambled into the small store.

"Senora," he politely addressed the woman behind the counter, "see that job over there?" Jorge pointed at the advertisement for the groomer position. "You know anything about that? Who owns that ranch? Or anybody who works there?"

The bodega owner, or at least Jorge assumed she was the owner, moved fluidly from behind the counter. A colorful, ankle-length skirt covered partially by a loose shirt that looked like it would fit a person several sizes larger than the woman wearing it made it impossible to discern the shopkeeper's true shape. Slender brown toes, adorned with bright red polish and enclosed in worn huaraches peeped from beneath the skirt's scalloped hem. A manicured hand brushed an errant strand of wavy, black hair to its proper place as the woman walked to examine the job posting. Jorge hadn't paid the woman much attention earlier when he used her phone, but seeing her now, he realized what had been bothering him since he walked back inside the bodega. The clothes she wore might fit the environment, but the woman's manicured hands, polished toes and coiffed hair did not. The incongruence reminded Jorge of a girl playing dress-up or a costume donned for a masquerade party.

"Is this who you called?" the woman asked, turning dark eyes toward Jorge.

"*Sí.* Do you know this place?" Jorge wondered what sort of answer he would hear.

"Yes. That is Senor McIntosh's ranch," the woman paused, seemed to consider a further answer but offered nothing else.

Jorge didn't like the woman's hesitation, or what he thought was her reluctance to provide more information about his new employer. "Is he a criminal?" Jorge watched the woman's eyes for the truth.

"No," the woman replied. "He's a good man. Work hard and he'll reward your efforts."

If Sean McIntosh wasn't a criminal, Jorge figured it wouldn't be any worse working for the Scotsman than any of the other ranchers or farmers he had encountered in the past fifteen years he had toiled in the fields. Still, information was always useful. "How do you know him?" Jorge pressed.

If he had not been watching closely, Jorge would have missed the shadow that quickly passed across the shopkeeper's face. In that fleeting instant, Jorge thought he caught sight of a different woman—a woman more at home in a fine hacienda, the sort of woman who would have considered him the hired help, a woman who carried an aura both of despair and high birth.

"It is not important," the woman replied with a forced smile. "If he is coming for you, it is better for you to wait outside."

The unspoken words hidden in the shopkeeper's dismissal picked at the edges of Jorge's mind. She would not share her story with him yet, but she would eventually. Jorge could be a patient man when he needed to be. The woman was a mystery that he was determined to solve.

CHAPTER SIX

Present Day

Warm sunshine caressed Allison's back while she watched her daughter, Charlotte, take the Appaloosa through its paces. Overlook Riding Club was a fancy name for the equestrian school owned and operated by Marion Hutcheson and her partner Jeri Kennedy. Located outside the Fort Charles city limits, and a scant fifteen minute drive from Allison's home, Overlook Riding Club offered riding instruction to students of all ages. Students could "rent" horses from the club or board their own for an additional fee. In addition to basic horsemanship, Marion and Jeri coached several serious students in competitive dressage.

Horses had been a way of escape for Allison growing up. Hours spent in the barn or riding her American Paint, Roscoe, had helped Allison maintain a sense of normalcy in her otherwise dysfunctional home. When, at the age of five, Charlotte began petitioning for a pony Allison gladly purchased a small Shetland and was grateful that Charlotte's wish was based on fascination with those magnificent creatures and not a need to escape from a terrible home life. Mack had followed his sister's footsteps for a few years, so Shetland number two arrived, but Tee-ball and flag football eventually replaced her son's interest in ponies.

Six years later, the ponies had a cushy life at the farm, Allison and Jim's home. Treated to frequent carrots and sugar cubes, the little ponies had plenty of attention but were seldom ridden anymore by their young owners. Charlotte had set her sights on competitive riding—and a new horse. Allison and Jim had purchased the Appaloosa two years earlier as a birthday present for their daughter. Named Diamond Girl by Charlotte in honor of the mare's forehead marking, the horse and child had become practically inseparable. Even when not taking a lesson, Charlotte could be found at the stables talking to or grooming her horse.

"Much better, Charlotte." Marion Hutcheson's strong voice drew Allison's attention. "That's enough for today. Take care of your horse now, while I have a chat with your mom about Asheville."

Jumping from her perch on the fenced surround, Allison followed Marion's nod directing her to the far side of the ring. "What's up?" Allison called to Marion when she was close enough not to have to yell.

"Hey, Allison." Marion offered a calloused hand in greeting. "I wanted to talk to you about the show in Asheville, North Carolina, that's set for next month. I think Charlotte's ready."

"Yeah, Charlotte's mentioned it to me already." Allison smiled. "I told her it would depend on her grades this period. Her report card should be in by next Friday. Will that give you enough time to get her registered?"

Marion responded with a laugh. "You can't tell me that child has anything but straight As. I've never seen such focus in a child her age."

"You're right," Allison agreed, "but we don't want her to think she can have everything just because she asks for something. Jim and I think it's important for our children to work for a goal, even if like in Charlotte's case it's pretty easy for them."

"Actually, I've already signed her up," Marion admitted sheepishly. "I figured you and the judge wouldn't object. Besides, the money isn't due for another ten days, so we're slick."

Walking back to the barn, Allison listened while Marion shared her thoughts on Charlotte's chances at the Asheville event, as well as her plans for other later competitions. Listening to Marion's assessment, Allison knew she had found the right teacher for her daughter.

"Say, Marion, let me change the subject a bit. What do you know about the thoroughbred farms down in north Florida?" Allison queried. "You or Jeri have any contacts down there?"

"I think Jeri is probably more knowledgeable than I am," Marion offered. "She worked for one of the larger breeders near Ocala before I met her. Why do you ask?"

Purposely vague, Allison replied, "One of the firm's client's has expressed an interest in raising thoroughbreds. I don't know much about that side of the horse business other than that Florida is one of the three states in the country where most thoroughbreds are registered—California and Kentucky being the other two. It just occurred to me while we were talking that you might know some of the people in the business there."

"I think Jeri's in the office." Marion headed into the open barn beckoning for Allison to follow. "Let's see what she might know."

Overlook's business office was little more than a glorified tack room just to the left of the barn's main entrance. Two oak desks that had seen much better days sat at ninety-degree angles to each other. Stacks of papers crowded the small top of the desk nearest the door, while its partner sat uncluttered and somewhat forlorn. "I don't know how she can find a damn thing on that desk," Marion observed.

"I'm sitting right here," Jeri advised her partner. "It's rude to talk about someone in front of them."

Marion leaned across the desk, causing the stack of papers nearest to the edge to flutter to the floor. "You know I love you." She smiled, planting a kiss on Jeri's lips. "Allison has a question."

Watching the play between the two women, Allison was convinced once again that opposites really did attract. Slight of build and delicate of bone, Jeri Kennedy could have passed for a teenager instead of the thirty-something she was. Light brown hair, tinged with blonder streaks, capped a pale, freckled face, which was highlighted by a lush, ripe mouth that always sported a shade of deep rose lipstick. Although clad in jeans, a plaid work shirt, and cowboy boots, Jeri still looked as though she had walked off the page of a fashion magazine. Allison wished she knew how Jeri did it. Marion, on the other hand, with her calloused hands, long dark hair hanging down her back in a messy braid, and aged overalls seemed the most unlikely match for Jeri that Allison could imagine. However, Allison knew the women had been together for almost ten years and had married in Vermont two summers earlier.

"How are you, Allison? It's good to see you. How can I help you?" Jeri asked.

Repeating the story she had told Marion, Allison continued. "My client asked me if I knew anything about one of the breeding farms, a place called McIntosh Farms. Like I told Marion, I don't really know much about the thoroughbred business, and I wondered if either of you did."

"It's been a while since I left Florida," Jeri began. "I don't remember any breeders near Ocala named McIntosh or any farms by that name either. Not that I knew all of them—the people I worked for had retired from the business about the time they hired me. All I did was take care of two of the mares they still had."

"Jeri wasn't there that long either," Marion interjected. Glancing at her partner, Marion asked, "We met about a year after you'd been there, isn't that right?"

Nodding, Jeri continued. "Yes, that's right. I started with the Johnsons in 2003, Marion and I met around the beginning of 2004, and by the end of that year, I'd left Ocala and moved up here with Marion."

"What are you trying to find out?" Marion turned her attention to Allison. "If your client has expressed an interest in getting into the horse business, surely he or she has already done the necessary homework on the industry. In fact"—Marion shook her head—"your client better have deep pockets as well. Thoroughbred breeding and racing is a very expensive way to earn a living."

"Oh, he has," Allison fibbed. "I'm simply trying to educate myself so I can better advise my client."

Jeri motioned toward one of the folding chairs near her desk. "Make yourself comfortable," she advised Allison. "I'll give you the ten-minute overview. Coffee?"

"Had too much already this morning." Allison declined the caffeine infusion, settled into the rickety seat, and waited.

"Although the term *thoroughbred* is sometimes used to refer to any purebred horse, it technically refers to only the breed of horse that is used in horse racing," Jeri began. "The thoroughbreds that we see today were developed in seventeenth- and eighteenth-century England and were the result of cross-breeding with Arabian and other Oriental stallions. The resulting breed was imported into North America starting in 1730 and today is found worldwide. If I recall correctly, over one hundred thousand foals were recorded last year, and almost forty thousand of those were in this county." Jeri moved aside a stack of papers to retrieve a half-empty bottle of Evian from the corner of her desk. Taking a long sip, the horsewoman added, "That's a lot of money and potential for more."

"Very interesting," Allison observed, "but how did Florida end up as one of the top breeding states? I thought Kentucky had a lock on that."

"Kentucky is still a big player in the industry," Jeri replied. "The thoroughbred sales in Keeneland bring in hundreds of millions of dollars each year for breeders from all over the country. There are several big horse farms in Kentucky, but over the years, Florida, California, and New York have edged right on up there."

"So where's the money best made in that business?" Allison asked. "Those horses don't race more than a couple of years."

"It's a combination of wins and stud fees," Jeri explained. "The more a horse wins, the higher priced his stud fee becomes. Bloodlines count, too—having a winner in several generations raises the horse's value, but it's important for the horse to win. A winner with a good pedigree can demand as much as half a million at stud."

"Good Lord." Allison was impressed. "I had no idea."

"You have to remember, though, that this is an expensive business to maintain," Jeri interjected. "There's a lot of money to be made, but any breeder will tell you, it's not a business for the faint of heart or someone who doesn't have really deep pockets."

Allison glanced at her watch. Charlotte should be finished rubbing down her horse by now, and Allison needed to get back for Mack's ball game at 4:00 p.m. Saturdays were busy in her family. "Thanks for the info, Jeri. All good stuff to know."

"Any time, Allison," Jeri replied with a grin. "And I'll make a call for you, see what I can find out about McIntosh Farms. I've still got some friends in Florida."

"That'd be great," Allison thanked her friend. "If you find out anything, just give me a call."

Driving home, Allison reflected on everything Jeri had shared. Whoever owned McIntosh Farms had to have money or at least a source for money. Frank was a good PI, but someone with the kind of money Allison suspicioned was necessary to run a thoroughbred horse farm could likely afford someone other than a relatively small-time investigator from Fort Charles, Alabama. Even more baffling was the fact that Frank would be working a case out of Florida. Allison had never even heard of the town the Florida secretary of state had listed as the locale for McIntosh Farms. Returning her attention to family matters, Allison knew she had her work cut out for her. Monday would come soon enough.

CHAPTER SEVEN

I t was hard for Frank to tell how much time had passed. The fat guy on the bed hadn't opened his eyes once since Frank had been watching him, but he had started to move around a bit in the last little while—or what seemed like a little while to Frank. Actually, Frank wasn't sure whether it was night or day, much less how long he'd been watching Mr. Fatty. The shades in the fat guy's room were always closed, and with the *beep, beep, beep* of that crazy machine with lights all over it, Frank finally decided maybe the fat guy wasn't supposed to wake up. But if that were the case, why did the people who kept coming in and out of the room talk about the fat guy coming out of a coma? None of this made any sense, especially because everyone seemed to think the fat guy was Frank. If Frank knew anything, he for sure knew he wasn't that fat slob lying on the narrow white hospital bed.

The creak of an opening door drew Frank's attention away from Mr. Fatty. "Thank you for coming," Frank heard the voice he had come to associate with the young teenager in doctor's whites. Deciding to get a closer look, Frank found himself hovering next to Mr. Fatty's bed.

"Jim and I will do anything we can to help." Frank noticed his friend Allison had entered the room. "I don't understand why Frank hasn't woken up yet. You said his body had healed almost completely from the gunshot wounds, and I thought the same was true of his surgical recovery."

"You are correct." Dr. Lopez nodded. "Mr. Martin's body is healthy. His recovery from the removal of that portion of his stomach and his spleen are right on target. If he was awake, he'd of course be under medical restrictions. But all in all from a medical point of view, Mr. Martin is having an excellent recovery."

"But?" Allison questioned as she approached the man on the bed. "It's been almost ten days now since Frank was placed in a coma. I know the drugs that had induced the coma were withdrawn after the third day postsurgery. Why hasn't he awakened?"

"We don't know." Dr. Lopez walked to the other side of the hospital bed to face Allison. "Some things in medicine are simply beyond our expertise. Coma, unfortunately, is sometimes one of those things." Shaking her head and skimming the man's chart, Dr. Lopez continued. "There is no medical reason for Mr. Martin to still be in a coma. None. On occasion, the voice of a family member can arouse a coma patient sufficiently to allow him or her to begin a return to consciousness."

"And Jim and I are the closest Frank has to family, is that your thinking, Doctor?" Allison interjected.

"Exactly," Dr. Lopez replied. "In the past twenty-four hours, Mr. Martin has begun to show some agitation. This is a hopeful sign and something we hoped to benefit from by having you or your husband begin to talk with Mr. Martin and to encourage him to wake up."

"Actually tell him to wake up?" Allison asked.

"Yes, and if Mr. Martin is used to taking orders from you, even better." Dr. Lopez smiled. "I've heard about some of the work you and Mr. Martin have done together. I think he'll respond to your voice—maybe not immediately, but I think you're the best shot we've got. Maybe the only shot."

"What do you mean, 'maybe the only shot'?" Allison asked with alarm.

"Generally, and most often, coma is associated with brain injury. The longer the patient is unconscious and the lower the patient falls on the Glasgow Coma Scale—eyes opening, verbal responses, and motor responses—the more likely it is that the person will never awaken, or if he does, that he will have permanent, and perhaps debilitating, disabilities." Dr. Lopez paused, raising her hand to halt Allison's interruption. "Mr. Martin's coma was caused by a carefully regulated dose of sedation medication which was withdrawn over a period of thirty-six hours beginning the third day after his surgery. Under normal circumstances, Mr. Martin should have returned to awareness four days ago."

"So why hasn't he?" Allison pressed.

"Again, we don't know." Dr. Lopez shrugged. "Something is holding him back, something that medical science doesn't understand. If Mr. Martin doesn't regain consciousness, we'll need to move him to a skilled nursing facility for long-term care."

"A nursing home? You'd send Frank to a freakin' nursing home?" Allison could barely control her outrage. "You and your staff put him in this condition, and you're just going to dump him out because you can't figure out why he won't wake up?" Donning her fiercest courtroom face, Allison glowered at the young doctor. "I don't think so."

"We won't have a choice." Dr. Lopez stood her ground. "The federal health-care law that was enacted back in 2010 has totally changed the landscape. Mr. Martin's health insurance won't cover an extended stay here in the hospital if he remains in this condition. The hospital will be forced to move him to a skilled nursing facility."

"How long do I have," Allison asked, "before you try to cart Mr. Martin out of here and I have to sue you and the hospital?"

Quietly, Dr. Lopez replaced the medical file in the holder at the foot of the bed. "Twenty-four hours," she replied as she turned to leave the room. "Good luck."

Frank watched as Allison pulled her cell phone from her purse, punched a number, and held the phone to her ear. "Jim, it's worse that I thought. They're moving Frank to a nursing home this time tomorrow unless he shows signs of coming out of the coma those bastards put him in. I've got twenty-four hours to get that stubborn SOB awake." Frank couldn't hear what the judge was saying on the other end of the line, but Frank was familiar with the pacing exercise Allison was performing in Mr. Fatty's room. Allison was putting together a plan. "That's right, I think so," Allison told her husband. "Tell Charlotte and Mack I'll see them tomorrow afternoon. I'll send Donna a text and have her reschedule any clients I have down as well." Allison stopped her pacing, smiled, and added, "Love you, too. See you tomorrow."

Frank wished he knew why Allison would be so concerned about Mr. Fatty. She called him a son of a bitch, so Frank knew Allison wasn't very happy with the guy. Lord, he'd hate to be on the receiving end of Allison's temper. Mr. Fatty better watch out.

Allison sat tentatively on the side of the hospital bed. Taking the man's hand in both of hers, Allison cleared her throat, and bent down to speak into the sleeping man's ear. "Frank Martin, you'd better get your ass back in your body," she demanded, "and I mean *now*. I know you're out there somewhere watching this little play, and I don't find your behavior one bit amusing. You've scared the crap out of me, Jim, and a lot of other people. Fun and game time is over. Get back here right now."

Allison, why are you talking to Mr. Fatty? The scene in the hospital room was beginning to disturb Frank. *Allison,* Frank called again trying to get his friend's attention, *here, up here. I'm up here.*

She can't hear you. A comforting voice whispered. *Not unless you go back.*

Frank liked the voice. The voice felt good, although Frank couldn't imagine how a voice could have a feeling like this. It didn't matter. Frank wanted to hear more from the voice and turned to look for the source, but another more insistent voice called to him.

"Frank, we love you. Please don't leave us. I know you can hear me." Frank watched a tear roll down Allison's face. "Come back to us. Please."

You must decide, the voice caressed Frank. *All have free choice.*

Why is she talking to that fat man? Frank asked the voice. He knew the voice held the answer to that question. *Why does she keep calling him by my name?*

Look closer, the loving voice suggested, *and see.*

As Frank considered the suggestion, he found himself immediately beside the sleeping man. Examining the stranger's features, Frank felt a nudge of memory. The more he looked at Mr. Fatty, the more the guy looked familiar. Time, if it existed at all, moved fluidly for Frank as he watched Allison alternate between berating the man in the bed for not waking up and then crying over Mr. Fatty's refusal to cooperate. Frank had just about decided the fat man wasn't worth his time when he heard a loud, disruptive bleat emanate from Mr. Fatty's body.

"Jesus Christ, Frank," Allison exclaimed. "If you're gonna fart like that, you better damn well wake up."

It's me, Frank thought, and he awoke.

CHAPTER EIGHT

Weekdays were almost as busy as Saturdays now. Morning lessons started at ten for preschoolers, with adult offerings for the leisure class at eleven and one thirty. Through trial and error, and actually running off a few clients, Marion and Jeri had figured out that women responded much better to Jeri. Marion thought it because she just looked too butch, but Jeri said no, it was just that she, Jeri, had a softer approach. So, even though teaching three classes in a row to youngsters and dilettantes made her want to pull her hair out on occasion, Jeri had added that task to her already-busy schedule as accountant and general manager of Overlook Riding Club.

The weekday after-school crowd was more serious. Time and money had a way of culling out those who were learning to ride solely for social status from those who had a serious passion for the sport. Marion's no-nonsense approach didn't bother the serious students one bit, no matter their age. By the time the first car arrived around three o'clock, Jeri was happily ensconced in the office, and Marion had taken over the riding ring. Saturdays were reserved for horse shows and one-on-one classes for advanced students. Marion and Jeri shared duties on that day, working with the student who responded best to each woman's method of teaching, whether in the practice ring or during competitions.

This particular Saturday had been especially busy. With the Asheville show only a week away, Marion and Jeri had spent the day working with the three students who would be representing Overlook in the dressage competition. Five o'clock had come and gone before the last of the students waved good-bye from the back seat of his mother's SUV.

"I had totally forgotten about my promise to Allison," Jeri remarked as she followed her partner from the barn. "I remembered the minute I saw her today and right before she asked me if I'd found out anything."

"I didn't think it was that big a deal," Marion replied. "Did Allison say something to you I don't know about?" Marion climbed the few steps leading up to the wide porch that wrapped the couple's log home, threw herself into a big Adirondack chair, pulled off dusty cowboy boots, and sighed. "Man, does this ever feel good."

"You remember Frank Martin? That PI Allison works with some?" Jeri stretched out on the green metal glider which was situated between Marion's chair and its twin at the other end of the porch near the living room windows. "Somebody shot Frank a couple of weeks ago. Sheriff Trowbridge asked Allison to take a look at some of Frank's current cases to see if anything stood out or rang a bell. They have no idea who the perpetrator might be, and Frank can't remember a thing about that night."

"And did it have something to do with what Allison asked about?" Marion asked.

"I specifically asked that very question today. All Allison said was that she was trying to track down every loose end, and the name Sean McIntosh and McIntosh Farms had come up in one of Frank's files." Jeri placed a foot on the floor to push the glider into a gentle rocking motion. "You know Allison. You can't get a darn thing out of that woman unless she wants to tell you. All she would say was that she wondered if anyone I knew in Florida in the horse business could give her some intel about the owner."

"Do you even know anyone who's still in the business down there?" Marion inquired. "I know I don't."

"I'll just have to call around and hope I get lucky," Jeri replied. "Allison's piqued my curiosity. She wouldn't be looking into this if she didn't have a good reason."

Pushing herself to a standing position, Marion groaned. "Lord, the longer I sit, the stiffer I get. Come on, sugar, let's clean up and run to town for supper tonight. You can make calls tomorrow. Sunday afternoon ought to be a good time to catch people at home."

Jeri's Gmail contacts list had proved her best source for names and phone numbers. Thank goodness she had thought to transfer the names and numbers from her old address book to the electronic version a couple of years ago. Jeri hadn't seen the original address book since and figured she'd likely thrown it out during one of her periodic purges. Of course, just as likely, the address book could be under one of the miscellaneous piles of paperwork on top, under, and around her desk. Purges occurred only about once a year and even then, not until Jeri's organizational skills, such as they were, reached overload.

The first two calls had proved unsuccessful, although enlightening. Teckla Blackwood, Jeri's friend from Rainbow Farms outside Ocala, had moved to Lexington, Kentucky, three years earlier to take a job at Keeneland, one of the country's premier racetracks and sales complexes for thoroughbreds. Jeri had forgotten all about Teckla's move until she noticed the 859 area code listed with Teckla's cell number.

"Sorry I can't help you," Teckla had apologized after the women had spent time catching up. "I don't remember any ranch called McIntosh Farms. Why don't you try Joanie and Brownie? They were still in Ocala when I left to come up here."

Like Jeri and Marion, Joanie and Brownie Teller were a pair, both professionally and romantically. Also, like Jeri and Marion, Joanie and Brownie appeared an unlikely match to outsiders and those who did not know the couple well. Augusta Johannes Bradley was born a Boston Brahmin, raised to take her place in a rarified part of society, destined to marry her male counterpart, expected to comport herself with the appropriate decorum, and admonished never to draw attention to herself.

Blake Jefferson Teller, aristocratic-sounding name notwithstanding, made his entrance into the world in a ramshackle sharecropper's house in the Mississippi Delta. Poverty was Brownie's only teacher, but he proved to be a quick learner. By the age of sixteen, Brownie had exchanged the rich, dark chocolate loam of the Delta for the sandy soils of north Florida, and that is when—at a dressage competition in Gainesville where Brownie was working as a stable hand and Joanie was showing her jumper Velvet—that fate introduced him to the girl destined to become his wife and soul mate.

It hadn't been easy for the two. Jeri remembered the story as she dialed the number Teckla had given her. Joanie's father had shipped her off to a finishing school in Switzerland and had threatened to have Brownie arrested on molestation charges. Two years had passed before the pair had been able to rendezvous in the States, and to the dismay of Joanie's parents the passage of time had only fanned the flames of young and unrequited love. Eighteen was the legal age for marriage in numerous states, a fact Brownie and Joanie took advantage of as soon as Joanie's years reached the magic number.

Brownie and Joanie had been fortunate. Young enough not to know much about the cruelties the world could impose and unafraid of hard work, the pair found employment in the horse ranches around Ocala. Brownie worked the stables, Joanie exercised the horses, and their employers provided room and board. By the time Joanie received a call from her grandmother's probate lawyer twelve years later informing her that she was now a rich woman, the couple had saved enough of their salaries to put a down payment on a small house.

The kind of money that Joanie inherited would have ruined a lot of people, but Joanie and Brownie barely changed their lifestyle. "It's nice to know we've got something to fall back on," Joanie had told Jeri once upon a time, "and we did use enough of Granmama's money to buy this ranch, but we've both seen the bad things money can do to people. We live on what we earn. That's plenty."

"You've reached Teller Landing. Please listen as our menu has changed. To schedule an appointment, press one. To hear a list of upcoming sales, press two. To speak with Joanie, press three. To hear this message again, press the pound sign," a pleasant but robotic voice informed Jeri.

Ha! Jeri thought. *Brownie's still got Joanie doing the front office work.* Punching the number *3* on her cell phone, Jeri hoped Joanie would answer on a Sunday afternoon.

"You've reached Joanie Teller. I'm either with a client or out in the barn. Please leave a message and I'll return your call when I can."

"Joanie, it's Jeri Kennedy. I hope you remember me," Jeri began.

"Jeri, what a surprise!" a happy voice interrupted Jeri. "What in the world are you doing, girl? And where are you?"

"Joanie, is that you?" Jeri replied. "I wasn't sure I'd get an answer on the Sabbath."

"Since when did anyone in this business rest on the Sabbath?" Joanie laughed. "I just let calls go to voice mail on Sundays, but I was in the office and heard your message start. God, it's good to hear your voice. How in the ever lovin' daylights are you and Marion?"

"Good, we're good," Jeri replied. "I apologize for letting so much time pass without touching base with you and Brownie. Teckla Blackwood gave me your number earlier today, and so here I am, calling you to catch up and to ask for some information."

"Is the information business related?" Joanie asked. "If so, let's get that out of the way."

"Yeah, it's related to the horse business but not specifically to our business," Jeri explained, continuing to share with Joanie the information Allison had discussed with her. "I told Allison I'd see if any of my Florida contacts knew anything about McIntosh Farms in Bell, or about a guy named Sean McIntosh who we assume is the owner of the place."

"I've got a vague recollection of a ranch with that name, but I can't recall much more than that it rings a distant bell, no pun intended," Joanie replied with a laugh. "Tell you what. The man you need to talk to is Plato McCall."

"Who is Plato McCall?" the name was new to Jeri.

"Well, Plato's an interesting guy. I knew him growing up in Boston. He got in some trouble, did some time in prison for white-collar crime and then several years later for some sort of fight with his sister, but he's been out now for a couple of years and seems to have gotten his act together," Joanie explained. "He's still got money. Lots of it from what I hear," the woman continued. "He bought a small horse ranch near Gainesville about a year ago."

"Why do you think I should talk to Plato?" Jeri wondered why her friend would suggest she speak to someone relatively new to the business and an ex-con to boot.

"Bell isn't that far from Gainesville. If there is anything to know about the ranches or farms in that area, I figure Plato would know. That man has had his fingers in more pies than you could count ever since he was a tad higher than a grasshopper," Joanie continued. "That's part of what landed him in jail the first time. If there is something to know about McIntosh Farms or Sean McIntosh, you can bet Plato will either know or be able to find out. Just tell him I gave you his number."

Twenty minutes later and after promising to stay in touch, Jeri thanked Joanie for her help and disconnected the call. The clock on the wall of the tack room showed almost 6:00 p.m., early suppertime for lots of folks. Jeri wondered whether she should take a chance in calling Plato McCall at this time of the evening. The afternoon's calls, while certainly turning out to be an enjoyable chat with old friends, had unfortunately rendered no information of any sort about McIntosh Farms. Jeri decided to take a chance. Maybe the third time would be the charm.

CHAPTER NINE

One Year Ago

The sweat stung his eyes, salty liquid spilling over his lower lids and running down the side of his nose, but the horse on the end of the lead demanded both of Jorge's hands and all of his attention.

"Easy, boy, easy," Jorge spoke softly to the agitated horse. Devil's Own Demon was McIntosh Farms' latest acquisition, and Jorge was positive that the stallion's name was a perfect fit. Thoroughbreds were high strung. Anyone in the business knew that, and Jorge was no exception. In the past couple of years that he had worked for Sean McIntosh, Jorge had learned to be both respectful and firm when dealing with the horses under his care. With a natural ease around horses, Jorge had found his work at McIntosh Farms to be hard but rewarding and Sean McIntosh a decent employer. All of the thoroughbreds at the farm had responded well to Jorge once they had become accustomed to his voice and touch—all of them except this new one.

"How's he doing?" Sean McIntosh climbed the wooden fence enclosing the exercise ring and planted himself on the top rail.

"Better, senor, but he is still dangerous. What happened to him?" Jorge asked.

"Just born ornery, best I can tell," Sean McIntosh surmised. "That one comes from a long line of winners. With the right trainer, he'll bring home some big purses." McIntosh fell silent. Watching his horses was an exquisite pleasure for him, a pastime the Scotsman never tired of. When he had seen Devil's Own Demon at the Keeneland sales earlier in the year, Sean McIntosh knew he had to have him. The horse had been expensive—$297,000—but given the colt's bloodline, McIntosh was certain he'd recoup that investment several times over.

"I'm interviewing a possible trainer next week," McIntosh told Jorge. "Guy by the name of Andrew Sutter. "

An involuntary shudder passed over Jorge causing him to surreptitiously make the sign of the cross.

Andrew Sutter had a bad name among local ranch workers. "Why Senor Sutter?" Jorge asked. Surely his boss had heard the same rumors.

"Sutter's well connected. He's backed several winners over the past few years. I've heard some bad things about him," McIntosh added, seeing the expression on Jorge's face, "but his win record is superb. I'm willing to give him a shot. You know Danny gave me his notice last week. I need to get someone in here pretty quick. I think I've found a dam to breed Demon with. Going down to see her next week. Name's Blue Scarlet. I'd like to take the new trainer with me."

Jorge nodded, keeping his attention on the black stallion. He knew better than to argue with his employer or to ask too many questions. Decent or not, Jorge knew there were some lines he couldn't cross with Sean McIntosh. Questioning who got hired at McIntosh Farms was one of those lines. Hiring a new trainer wasn't the problem. Trainers were hired and fired regularly in the horse racing business. Those whose horses won kept their jobs. Those with too many losses on the track found themselves out of a job. Jorge and Danny Morgan, the trainer who was leaving, had begun to develop a friendship and Jorge hated to see Danny go. However, turnover, whether voluntary or not, was just part of the profession.

Andrew Sutter, on the other hand, was something else entirely, a something else that brought old memories, memories Jorge would rather have forgotten, to the forefront of his mind.

Jorge was not a particularly superstitious man. Sure, he attended church fairly regularly, more from the habit of his Catholic upbringing than any true need for spiritual guidance, but beyond that, Jorge had tried to dismiss and forget the teachings of his childhood in Guatemala. Most folk in westernized countries assumed that Mayan folklore and religious customs had faded with the Spanish conquistadors. After all, Guatemala was a modern country with almost 80 percent of its population identifying on census forms as Catholic. The capital, Guatemala City, was internationally known as a political and cultural center. What many people didn't know, unless they happened to be history majors, was that modern Guatemala once formed the core of the great Mayan civilization. Hundreds of years after the Spanish invasion of South America and the disappearance of the Mayans, the lingering overtones of both the Mayan religion and culture continued to infiltrate and shape much of Guatemalan life, especially in the barrios and poorer regions of the country. There, the Jesus of Christianity was known just as easily as the Sun God, while his mother, Mary, often assumed the identity of the Moon Goddess.

Long before the US Congress brought equal rights into the collective vocabulary of most of the world, the Mayan religion offered equal opportunity to both men and women, allowing either sex to officiate in religious ceremonies. The Mayan priest, or shaman, held a position of great power. Able to bargain with the unknown forces that governed human destiny, shamans were believed to predict the future and to cast spells. A shaman who possessed the power to heal could also claim the title of *curandero/curandera*, or healer. Jorge's grandmother Rosaria had been known by both.

The gift is passed generation to generation. Jorge heard his *abuela*'s voice in his head. *Your mother, may the goddess bless her soul, did not want to accept her destiny. Her refusal of the gods' gift brought their wrath upon her.* Jorge shook his head; he did not want to remember what Rosario had told him. *You are the gifted one now. Accept your path.*

Leaving Guatemala, turning his back on the superstition that had enveloped and destroyed his mother, Jorge had been able to ignore his grandmother's words for almost a decade. But his employer's mention of the name Andrew Sutter had shattered the carefully constructed illusion Jorge had created for his life. Gifted or not, believing in the old ways or not, Jorge had been unable to ignore the fact that he knew things before they happened, and moreover that he saw evil people for what they were no matter how upstanding and righteous they might appear to the casual observer. And by saw, Jorge meant really saw—with the facade of skin ripped from bone to reveal a dark, writhing mass of blackness. Andrew Sutter was one of those people.

CHAPTER TEN

Present Day

Soft foods—Frank was sick to death of soft foods. Glancing over the discharge papers Dr. Lopez had given him, Frank snorted in disgust at the meals that had been included by the hospital's dietitian. *Who in blazes can live on this crap?* Frank conversed silently with himself. Soft boiled eggs, toast, Jell-O—at least that stuff looked like food. Having to puree his vegetables in a food processor was disgusting. And no fried food. Frank decided he'd rather be dead than be denied fried chicken or barbecue ribs. *To hell with it*, Frank decided, tossing the neatly typed pages from UAB Hospital into the trash receptacle next to his desk.

"Mr. Martin?" a hesitant voice inquired. "You up for a visitor?"

"Maybe," Frank replied gruffly. "Who is it?"

"It's me, Frank," Allison pushed her way past Frank's receptionist. "It's time you quit ignoring my calls. You and I are gonna have a talk." Allison hurried around Frank's desk and placed a gentle kiss on the man's balding head before her friend could utter a word in response. "You've been home almost a week now, and that's where you still ought to be— not here in this office."

"How'd you know I was here?" Frank's tone implied a degree of pissed-offness that Allison recognized.

"Don't get your panties in a wad, Frank," Allison retorted. "I told Sheila to call me if you showed up before the fifteenth. I know Dr. Lopez told you to continue bedrest until then, and after that, just to start back half days." Motioning to the stack of files littering Frank's desk, Allison continued. "That doesn't look like half-day work to me, and it sure isn't the fifteenth of the month yet."

A loud screech rolled out of Frank's office chair as he tipped his considerable girth backward, allowing the chair's spring mechanism to tilt the seat and its occupant toward the wall behind Frank's desk.

"I'm not gonna be babysat by Sheila or you," Frank huffed.

"Nobody's babysitting you, Frank." Allison struggled not to laugh at Frank's sulky retort. "You had a close call and scared everyone who loves you. No one wants you to end up back at UAB because you're too stubborn to follow doctor's orders. We're just trying to protect you from yourself."

Frank's chair continued its screech, although at a lower decibel and slower pace than previously, while Frank studied his office ceiling. Allison waited patiently. She and Frank had been friends for too many years for her not to recognize the scene in front of her. Frank was trying to decide whether to share information with her. Finally, tipping the desk chair to an upright position, Frank rested his elbows on his desk and turned dark gray eyes toward Allison.

"I can't sit at the house any longer. I'm restless, discontented, irritable—feels sometimes like I'm being run over by a bunch of ants." Frank shook his head. "I had Sheila bring my active case files out to the house after I got home. I've looked through all of them trying to get a glimpse of what took me out to the Anderson place that night. Nothing—absolutely nothing. I can't remember a damn thing," Frank explained. "I thought maybe if I came back into the office, got back in a regular routine, that something would pop, I'd remember some small detail that would bring my memory back."

"Has anything worked?" Allison asked.

"All I've done is find a blank wall from the day before I got shot until I woke up in the hospital. How am I going to find out who did this to me and why?" The pain in Frank's voice echoed in his words.

Allison reached across the desk to clasp Frank's hands. "Do you remember anything about a guy named Sean McIntosh?"

"I saw that name in one of my files," Frank replied. "I have no idea who that is, or why I have a file on him and a place called McIntosh Farms." But a small nudge began to move in the periphery of Frank's brain. Was that a memory? "Do you know anything about that file?" he asked.

"Toby called the number you had written in the file. He talked to a man named Sean McIntosh who claimed he is your cousin, albeit a pretty distant one. McIntosh told Toby he'd retained you to find a stolen horse." Allison paused. "Does any of that ring a bell?"

Frank closed his eyes and commanded his brain to search, but all that appeared was the black wall, and wait...something else. Something soothing, comforting, welcoming. Frank's mind reached for the faint memory, but like a wisp of smoke caught on the tail of a breeze, whatever had been at the edge of

Frank's recall had vanished into the ether. "There's something, but I can't get a hold of it at all. I don't think it's related to this case either, but it seems familiar somehow." Frank shook his head. "You're right, though. I'm tired and I probably shouldn't have come in today. All of a sudden I'm plum worn out."

"Come on, then. I'll give you a ride home," Allison offered. "And please follow doctor's orders for a few more days. Your office will still be here next week, and so will your clients."

The sun was setting when Frank woke up from his nap. Allison had been right. He was pushing himself too hard too soon. And on top of that, Frank wasn't a young man anymore, a fact Frank knew intellectually but had a hard time accepting at a gut level. Once upon a time, looking in the mirror had been just a routine part of his day when he shaved or brushed his teeth. Now it was like a trip to the house of horrors. Who was that old man who stared back at Frank each morning? Well, there was nothing that could be done to change what was, that Frank knew for sure.

Ambling slowly into his kitchen, Frank decided a PB and J would do just fine with a cold glass of milk.

Best he could tell, this was the kind of soft food meal he could eat and enjoy. Two sandwiches and one bowl of vanilla ice cream later, Frank poured a cup of coffee and moved to the den. He'd been thinking about Sean McIntosh's claim of kinship, and the more Frank had thought about it, the stronger came a little, persistent itch in the back of his brain.

Frank's parents had died when he was ten years old. Although raised by loving foster parents, almost all of the personal items from Frank's birth family had disappeared with his entrance into the foster care system. The bookcase near the TV held his mother's old photo albums, one of the few items from his real family that Frank's foster parents had saved for him. It had been years since Frank had looked at the albums. When Frank had moved into his current digs, he'd simply shoved them onto the top shelf and forgotten about them. Draining the last sip of coffee, Frank set aside the cup and reached for the album that was the easiest to fetch.

The next couple of hours passed quickly. More than once Frank laughed so hard that tears came to his eyes. The pictures and the memories they recalled were mostly hilarious and some sad, but whether funny or sorrowful, they were well worth the evening's time. Frank had totally forgotten about the reason he had started looking at his mother's old pictures when he opened the cracked leather album marked "1965." Knock-kneed and reed thin, with blondish hair in the popular buzz cut of the 1960s, Frank's five-year-old self stood grinning, his left arm wrapped around the shoulder of a boy of similar size. Sliding the worn black-and-white photo from its cellophane cover, Frank flipped the picture over. There, in his mother's prim handwriting were the words *Frank and Sean. May 18, 1965.*

"Well, I'll be damned," Frank whispered. Then he reached for the phone.

CHAPTER ELEVEN

Jim Kaufman's cardiologist shook his patient's hand, settled himself on the exam room's rolling stool, and gave the judge as serious look. "I got the results from the EKG you had last week. I don't like what I'm seeing."

"I feel fine, Larry. I'm sure it's nothing." Allison's husband had undergone regular electrocardiogram tests since his heart attack and stent eighteen months earlier. He'd been religious about following the diet and exercise Dr. Fuller had prescribed. "I feel better than I have in a long time," Jim tried to assure the specialist.

"You felt fine right up until you keeled over from your heart attack, remember? You're just one of those people who doesn't have any symptoms, any warning signs, that a heart event is imminent," Dr. Fuller explained. "Unfortunately for you, how you feel just isn't a good predictor of your cardiac health. The only way to follow you medically is with testing."

Jim knew what was probably coming, but he asked anyway. "So what's next? A nuclear stress test?"

Larry Fuller nodded. "I'll have my nurse call you later today with the appointment. I'd like to get this done as soon as possible."

The serious tone of his doctor's voice caught Jim by surprise. "Is there something you're not telling me, Larry?" he asked. "Why the rush for the stress test?"

"You're fifty-four years old, Jim, which is still relatively young, but you've already had one heart attack, you've got a stent, and now you've got a squirrely EKG. Allison would have my head if I ignored the results of the EKG and you ended up with another occlusion." Ushering his patient to the door of the exam room he added, "It's just a couple of hours out of your schedule. Better to be safe than sorry."

The afternoon passed quickly. Jim's court docket had included two arraignments on first-degree murder charges, one arraignment on a domestic violence charge, and one arraignment on a drug-trafficking offense. Setting a bond on the drug case was fairly simple. This was the first offense for the twenty-year-old defendant who had experienced the misfortune of being pulled over for speeding with a couple of ounces of pot resting in a baggie in the open ashtray compartment next to the driver's seat. The amount of pot was what had resulted in the drug-trafficking charge even though the pot was most likely simply for the defendant's personal and recreational use. The judge knew the case would ultimately be concluded with a plea deal of community service and probation. The jails were simply too crowded to incarcerate someone on a minor drug charge. This defendant was no danger to society. Jim released him without bond on his own recognizance. If the boy was dumb enough not to appear at the next hearing, the judge would issue a bench warrant and not be so lenient the next time.

Before deciding on bond for the defendant charged with domestic violence, Jim turned to the desk-top computer at the edge of the bench and typed in a search command. The advent of electronic record keeping had greatly improved record retrieval, and the county commission's decision three years earlier to place a computer on the bench for each of the county's judges had been a stroke of genius. Jim was pretty certain this particular defendant had been in his court within the last year. A quick glance at the information filling the computer screen confirmed the judge's recall. This was the third time in twenty-four months that Sam Benton's wife had charged him with assault, resulting in his arrest by the Calhoun County Sheriff's Office. Over the protestations of Benton's court-appointed lawyer, Jim set bond at $10,000, an amount the judge knew would take a few days for Sam's wife or whoever else was bailing him out this time to gather. "Mr. Benton seems unable to comprehend the seriousness of his offenses, Counselor," the judge had explained. "Maybe a little cooling off period in the county jail will prove educational for your client."

The arraignments for the two men charged with murder were quick and to the point. Neither man was granted bond and both were quickly remanded to the prison cells where they had been spending the last several days. In keeping with state and federal guidelines for speedy trial, Jim also set trial dates for both defendants. As the last of the alleged murderers were led from the courtroom, the judge turned to address his bailiff. "Dickie Lee, I'm going to be out this Friday. Larry Fuller wants me to take a stress test. Why don't you go ahead and take an early weekend? I know you've been wanting to take Libby up to Gatlinburg."

Dickie Lee Bishop threw a worried look at his boss. He remembered all too well the day Judge Kaufman had collapsed with a heart attack during closing arguments of a criminal trial. Reaching the stricken jurist that morning, Dickie Lee had been sure Judge Kaufman was a dead man. Dickie Lee thought the judge had completely recovered. This news didn't sound that way. "Judge, are you OK?"

Jim Kaufman waved his hand dismissively. "I'm fine, Dickie Lee. Larry Fuller's just being overly cautious. There's nothing to worry about."

Dickie Lee knew Dr. Fuller. The doctor wasn't given to ordering unnecessary tests. No, if Dr. Fuller was ordering the judge to take a stress test, he had a good reason. "You tell Ms. Parker about this?" Dickie Lee hoped he wasn't being impertinent, but he was going to call the judge's wife himself if he needed to. The look Jim Kaufman gave his bailiff in reply had cowed many a litigant in the judge's courtroom. Dickie Lee flinched but returned the judge's stare. "Not meaning to overstep, Your Honor. Just knowing how your wife is, she'd be pretty angry if she thought you were keeping something from her." Taking a deep breath, the bailiff ventured a last observation. "And she'd never forgive me if I knew something she thought she ought to know and I didn't tell her."

"First Larry Fuller and now you," Jim exclaimed. "How is it that grown men are afraid of my wife? No, don't even attempt to answer that question." Jim shook his head with a laugh. "Don't worry, Dickie Lee. I plan to tell Allison tonight. I know she'll worry about this, and I need to tell her in person, not over the phone. It's just not the big deal you and Doc Fuller seem to think it is."

On the drive home an hour later, Jim reflected on the day's events. He really didn't think anything was wrong with his heart, but he'd be foolish not to take his doctor's concerns seriously. Jim would do the best he could to assuage what he knew would be Allison's immediate fears upon hearing the news. Yes, best to get this test behind him, reassure everyone that he was fine, and get on with his life. Jim had a lot of years ahead of him, and he intended to enjoy each and every one of them.

CHAPTER TWELVE

David Jackson whistled a tune he couldn't really place but which kept playing in his mind as he ambled from his office in the back corner of Parker & Jackson to Allison's sunny one closer to the front of the law firm. *What a great day to be alive.* David smiled, reflecting on the early morning lovemaking he and his wife, Sarah, had enjoyed before their busy day had started. The death of Sarah's father and David's old boss at Johnson & Merritt several years ago had been more blessing than sorrow, as odd as that might sound to an outsider. Sarah had grieved her father's passing, but the hard realities of Ben Johnson's double life had been the unlikely catalyst that launched Sarah on an inner journey of personal discovery and that had led, in time, to the renewal and deepening of David and Sarah's marriage. Opening Parker & Jackson had closed the circle for David in a way he had not contemplated but that he now acknowledged as the perfect union of his professional and personal lives. David was content.

"Hey, Allison. You got a minute?" David stuck his head around the open doorway of Allison's office.

Raising a finger, Allison shushed David and returned her attention to the caller on the other end of the phone she cradled between her ear and shoulder. "My client's position is fully supported by current case law. You know as well as I do that we'll obtain a defense verdict if this case is tried. Your client is wasting my time." David grinned as he watched Allison's face telegraph the response she was getting from opposing counsel. Catching her partner's eye, Allison rolled her own and used her free hand to mimic a mouth opening and closing. "Yes, I know, Matt, but a bird in the hand is better than a big fat zero, which is what a jury is going to award your client if you try this case. My client has a one-time offer on the table, solely to avoid the costs of litigation. Take it or leave it." David settled himself in one of Allison's comfortable client chairs and listened to his favorite litigator work on her opposition. "Let me know what your client decides, Matt. The offer's open until close of business tomorrow."

With the call concluded, Allison swiveled her desk chair to face David and sighed. "Whew, dealing with Matt Aiken is like taking a dose of prune juice. How the man gets clients is a mystery."

"What's the case about?" David inquired.

"Wrongful termination. Matt's client was the Human Resources director for Allied Plastics." Allison reached for the ever-present can of Coke Zero, took a sip, and then continued. "Get this— he was fired for sexual harassment." Seeing David's raised eyebrows, Allison laughed. "I know. You'd think he'd know better. Anyway, he claims his firing was just pretense, made-up so to speak, and that he was really fired for being a whistle-blower."

Whistle-blowing was the legal term used when an employee brought violations of laws to the attention of authorities. David knew there had been some pretty big jury awards in favor of employees who had been fired for being whistle-blowers. "You don't seem to think Matt's client has much of a case. Usually, these kinds of cases bring a good-size jury award for the fired employee." David leaned forward, interested in his partner's take on the case.

"There *is* some exposure for my client," Allison admitted. "The HR director engaged in some sure-enough sexual harassment at another of my client's facilities a couple of years ago. If I'd been representing Allied at the time, I would have recommended firing him then. Unfortunately, this guy had a friend in the corporate offices, so all he got was a write-up and some remedial training. Then last year, he was relocated to the operation in Eufala. That's when he got in trouble again."

"What had he done the first time?" David was intrigued. "It must have been pretty bad if you think he should have been fired."

Shaking her head, Allison explained, "This guy is white. His wife is African American—nothing wrong with that, but apparently because one woman of color loves him, this jerk thought he could say anything he wanted to about and to African American women. Here he was, the HR director, and he's telling African American women employees things like, 'I like my coffee like I like my women—hot and black' and 'Once you go black, you can't go back.'"

"Oh my God"—David nearly choked on the sip of coffee he had just taken—"what an idiot."

"Disgusting," Allison agreed. "But the problem now is that what he got fired for—kissing the hand of an African American security guard—that's so 'nothing' that I am a bit worried about convincing a jury that pretext doesn't apply. I've convinced Allied to put this settlement offer on the table, but if the plaintiff doesn't take it, I'll have to do my best to convince a jury that there was a legitimate reason for firing the guy, even though my client basically let him slide the last time when he did something much worse. If I were on a jury, I'm not sure I'd believe my own case."

"I've got to give it to you, Allison, I don't know how you deal with all that crazy stuff that comes out of some of these employment cases," David informed his partner. "Better you than me. Give me a good old personal injury case any day."

"Yuck!" Allison exclaimed. "Save me from dealing with insurance companies." Noticing the sheaf of papers David had brought with him to her office, Allison changed the subject. "Did you want to talk to me about a particular case?"

David noticed Allison's glance at the papers he had on his lap. "Oh, it's not about this," he explained, nodding toward the paperwork. "I wanted to talk to you about Frank, see what you had heard from Sheriff Trowbridge."

"Toby's not any closer today to discovering who shot Frank than he was a few weeks ago." Allison opened a side desk drawer and retrieved a slim, brown file folder. "I've got copies of the intake sheets for the cases Frank was working when he was shot. This one seems to have the most promise." Allison handed David a file marked "McIntosh Farms." "Frank called me late last night. He was going through some old family photo albums, trying to make sense of Sean McIntosh's claim that they are cousins, and he came across a picture of himself and another boy. The writing on the back of the photo says, 'Frank and Sean' and it's dated '1965.'"

David gave Allison a surprised look. "Then it's true? Frank and this guy are related? Surely, his own kin wouldn't shoot him?"

"Looks like the family connection is true, and I don't know why Frank's cousin would hire him and then try to kill him," Allison mused. "Frank's coming by later today to show me the picture. He still can't remember why Sean hired him, and all Toby has to go on is McIntosh's claim that he hired Frank to locate a stolen horse."

"Well, knowing you, I can see where this is going next," David surmised.

"Yes, a road trip seems appropriate," Allison replied, confirming David's suspicions. "I think Frank needs to see Sean McIntosh in person. Maybe an in-person conversation will shake loose some memories for Frank. Plus, I want to hear the whole story on this stolen horse business from Mr. McIntosh."

"Just do me a favor," David requested. "Get the sheriff's approval before you and Frank gallivant off to north Florida."

"Already on my to-do list," Allison assured her concerned partner. "Not to worry."

The last of supper's dishes had been loaded into the dishwasher, the cat fed, and Charlotte and Mack sent upstairs to take their respective baths before settling in for a family movie night. Although school wouldn't let out for the summer for another week, Allison knew her children had already mentally checked out of the academic routine. Plus, because nothing much transpired at the end of the semester for elementary-age students, Allison had acquiesced to her children's pleas for a midweek movie night with their parents.

"Charlotte and Mack want to watch *The Chamber of Secrets*—you know, one of those Harry Potter movies," she called to Jim who had already left the kitchen. "Think you can handle that?"

"If I can stay awake," Jim replied as Allison followed him into the comfortable den adjacent to the home's country kitchen. "I bet I'm asleep before Harry and the crowd get back to Hogwarts for the year."

Allison positioned herself strategically on the oversized sofa that faced a large stone fireplace, resting her head on one of the sofa's plush arms and her feet in her husband's lap. "I may beat you to it." She laughed. "It's been a long day. And speaking of days, I tried to get you this morning, but your secretary said you had gone to a doctor's appointment. I didn't see anything on our calendar about that." Allison cocked her head, giving Jim a look that demanded an honest answer.

"It's nothing." Jim affected a casual tone. "Larry Fuller called for a follow-up. He wants me to take another nuclear stress test." Seeing alarm spread across Allison's face, Jim rushed to add, "It's just a precaution, Allison. Larry says because I never have physical symptoms, he just wants to check me via testing."

"Have you had any chest pains?" Allison ignored Jim's comments. "Are you hiding something from me, Jim? I swear, if you are hiding something from me, you can rest assured I'll kill you before a heart attack will." Fear belied Allison's strong words.

Pushing Allison's feet aside, Jim moved to embrace his wife. "I'm fine, Allison," Jim whispered, placing a kiss on his wife's head. "I knew you'd worry, which is why I dreaded telling you this. But truly, it's just Larry Fuller being overly cautious. I'm fine, my heart is fine, and nothing is going to happen to me."

"When is the test?" Allison asked.

"This coming Friday," Jim replied. "Just routine."

The sound of running feet interrupted further conversation as Charlotte and Mack thundered into the den. Pushing aside more questions, Allison gathered her small family to herself. Tonight was movie night—popcorn and snuggling together on the sofa,

Allison and Jim cocooning Charlotte and Mack. Tomorrow, Allison promised herself, she would call Dr. Fuller and find out exactly what was going on with her husband.

CHAPTER THIRTEEN

Google maps claimed the most direct route from Fort Charles to Bell, Florida, would be a scant four-hour jaunt. Allison and Frank had left from their offices at seven that morning. Almost three hours had passed with Frank giving only a very un-Frank-like yes or no to every question Allison had posed about the attempt on his life. Allison had just about decided to give up on fruitful conversation when Frank commented, "Did you know the Appalachian Mountains are over three hundred million years old?"

"I knew they were old," Allison replied, wondering what the connection was between ancient mountains and an attempt on Frank's life. "Why do you ask?"

"Kinda hard to get your head around all that, isn't it?" Frank replied, not answering Allison's question. "Once, they were higher than the Himalayas, then they eroded to nothing. When the continents collided after the age of the dinosaurs, the Appalachians were lifted up again. Hard to think of all that happening so many millions of years ago." Frank tapped his fingers against the passenger window. "Those mountains have been raised up and then eroded to nothing twice. This last time they got raised up was about five million years ago. And three or four million years from now, they'll be eroded to nothin' again." Frank pushed the seat's recliner button in an attempt to garner more leg room. Riding in Allison's Miata was a tight squeeze for Frank. "Our lives are just a blink of an eye, if that."

Allison tossed a worried glance at her passenger. She had never heard Frank talk about anything remotely esoteric or morose. What was going on? "Frank, are you OK?" she asked.

A long sigh escaped Frank's lips, but a smile creased his face as he turned toward Allison. "I'm fine. Really, I am."

"Frank"—Allison's voice commanded her companion's attention—"what is it?"

"I had an experience I can't explain. When I was in the hospital"—Frank twisted his torso to face Allison as she drove—"I was above my body, but I didn't really think it was me. I saw you and the judge, listened to y'all talking to the doctor. I don't know how long I was there—time didn't seem to matter or even exist. I even tried to talk to y'all, to tell you I wasn't that guy in the bed, but y'all couldn't hear me."

Allison had heard of and read about out-of-body experiences, but she had never known anyone personally who claimed to have had one. "Were you frightened?"

"No," Frank quickly replied. "In fact, I felt great. Don't take this the wrong way, Allison, but I didn't want to come back."

"Then why did you?" Allison didn't know what to say other than to ask the obvious. If Frank thought this had happened to him, then Allison was going to honor his belief.

"There was this voice. It told me I had to choose," Frank explained. "And I really wasn't going to go back because I knew I wasn't that fat guy in the hospital bed that you were talking to. But then, when Mr. Fatty farted and you called him my name, I just knew the guy was me—and then all of a sudden I'm in that hospital room."

Allison laughed gently, remembering, then reached across the car's console to pat Frank's hand. "Frank, I don't know what you experienced, and I'm not saying it didn't happen. But whatever went on, I'm just glad you're back. What's important now is finding out who tried to kill you. And Sean McIntosh is our best lead."

Frank nodded. "I still don't have any memory of talking to Sean about the case he apparently hired me for."

"Toby said Sean was terrified when he told him you'd been shot, claimed he'd be the next victim. My gut tells me there's some link between the case you got hired on and what happened to you out at the old Anderson place," Allison remarked. "Whether we can get much out of your cousin remains to be seen."

"Oh, we'll get something, all right," Frank's replied gruffly. "Or I'll know the reason why."

The pair filled the remaining miles with small talk, Frank describing some of the old pictures he had come across in his mother's albums, Allison bringing Frank up to speed on her husband's latest medical testing. "Jim says there's no need to worry about this latest test, but I can't help but be nervous about it."

"Jim's fine," Frank assured Allison. "He can run circles around men half his age. Listen to the judge—don't worry about your husband."

The beginning of a black horse fence along the side of the highway caught Allison's eye at the same time her GPS announced, "Destination ahead, on left." Slowing the car, Allison turned into an asphalt driveway and drove underneath a large, iron arch with the words *McIntosh Farms* displayed over the entrance to the property. The driveway, wide enough to accommodate horse trailers and larger vehicles, was bordered on both sides by large paddocks where several horses grazed. Farther up the drive, in a rapidly approaching distance, stood several large barns and other buildings of unknown function. Near to the barns, Allison could see a training ring similar to the one at Overlook Riding Club, and beyond that, what appeared to be a regulation-size racing track.

"Nice setup," Allison remarked. "No one living in the cheap seats here."

"Hmm." Frank snorted noncommittally. "I never heard tell of any kin with this kind of money. I'll be interested to hear how my Scottish cousin is able to afford all this."

"Do I detect a hint of jealousy?" Allison asked mischievously, giving her companion an affectionate nudge.

"Nah," Frank replied. "Just a gut feeling and a lot of questions for my cousin, if that's who he really is."

Further conversation ceased as Allison's and Frank's attention was caught by the unmistakable sound of screaming coming from the barn where Allison had stopped. Throwing the car's transmission into park, Allison leaped from her car running beside Frank toward the barn's open doors. In the few seconds that it took for Allison's eyes to adjust to the barn's darkened interior, Allison heard Frank exclaim, "What the hell?" Taking a few steps forward, Allison noted in quick succession a man lying prostate on the barn floor, another man standing over him brandishing a whip, and a large black horse whose prancing and snorting telegraphed extreme agitation.

Acting on pure instinct and moving slowly so as not to draw unwanted attention, Allison reached inside her jacket and withdrew her GLOCK .26 from the shoulder holster she had begun to wear after nearly losing her life the previous year. "I don't know what's going on here, and I don't want to shoot the wrong person," Allison advised the standing man. "And I sure don't want to harm this gorgeous horse. So I suggest you lay down that whip and move over to that stall over there." Allison nodded at the man who had now lowered the whip, and pointing her gun toward the side of the barn, she indicated where the man should stand. "Frank, check that guy on the floor," Allison ordered. "I can't tell if he's dead or alive."

"He'll wish he was dead if he's harmed Demon," came a harsh promise from the man holding the whip. Detecting a heavy Spanish accent, Allison asked, "Who are you?"

"Jorge Velasquez. I work for Senor McIntosh."

"And who is that?" Allison directed her gaze at the man whom Frank was examining.

"An asshole." Contempt coated Jorge's words. Returning his attention to Allison and acknowledging the gun she still held, Jorge advised, "I need to calm Demon before he hurts himself."

When Allison nodded her assent, the dark-skinned man moved quietly and slowly toward the still-nervous horse. "*Calmarse, Diablo, calmarse,*" Jorge crooned. "*No se preocupe.*" A square sugar cube appeared in Jorge's outstretched hand. "*Azúcar, Diablo.*" The black horse tossed his head but stopped its prancing to eye the proffered treat. "It's fine now," Jorge announced in English, and to prove the veracity of his statement, the man clasped the horse's halter and led him to a nearby stall.

A soft moan drew Allison's attention. Frank had turned the other man onto his back. "He's alive but not really conscious," Frank remarked. "I don't think this is Sean McIntosh."

"Of course he isn't," an aggravated voice replied. "Lady, why are you pointing a gun at my ranch hand? And why is Andrew laid out on the floor?"

A man of indeterminate age stood just inside the barn's open doors. Silver haired, no taller than average height, the man's unlined skin marked a sharp contrast to his almost-colorless hair. He could have been fifty or seventy or somewhere in between. Puffing on a pipe clinched between his teeth, the man asked, "Well, is anyone going to answer my questions?"

Determining that whatever had been going on was now contained, Allison returned her gun to its holster. "I'm Allison Parker. This is Frank Martin. We're here to see Sean McIntosh, who I assume is you. When we got here, we heard screaming and ran in here to find your ranch hand standing over this guy. He had a whip in his hand, and I think he'd been using it on Andrew here."

"That so?" McIntosh asked Jorge, who having safely secured the black horse, had now returned to the middle of the barn.

"*Sí*, Senor McIntosh," Jorge admitted. "I caught him whipping Demon."

A deep scowl marred McIntosh's features. "Is he hurt?"

"No, senor. I stopped him in time." Jorge's answer confirmed Allison's suspicion that McIntosh's concern had been for the horse and not the man on the floor. "But, senor, I let my temper get the best of me. I have hurt Andrew."

"Andrew can go fuck himself," McIntosh replied. "As soon as he comes to, he can pack his bags and get the hell off my property." McIntosh pulled a small army knife from his pocket, tamped down the tobacco in his pipe with the blunt end, and then turned his attention to Frank Martin. "You've gotten fat as a tick, Frankie, me boy." The Scotsman grinned. "Glad to see they didna kill ye."

"Good to see you, too," Frank replied sarcastically. "Allison and I came a long way to see you. If all this drama's over, we'd like to hear about why you hired me, and why you think whoever tried to kill me is gonna come after you."

CHAPTER FOURTEEN

The main house at McIntosh Farms was low and rambling. Live oaks, hundreds of years old given their size, sheltered the house from the Florida sun, embracing the clapboard, ranch-style abode with large, gnarled branches from which hung long, gray strands of Spanish moss. A light breeze moved the moss, whispering through the branches of the ancient guardians, interspersing the limbs with shafts of filtered sunlight.

The somewhat run-down appearance of Sean McIntosh's house seemed out of place with the pristine barns, outbuildings, paddocks, and other accoutrements apparently needed to run a top-notch horse farm. Allison pondered the significance of what this incongruity might reveal about Sean McIntosh. If their accommodations were any indication, the horses at McIntosh Farms lived a lot better than their owner did.

"We'll sit out here," Sean McIntosh advised his guests, motioning for Allison and Frank to take a seat on the house's veranda. "Been without a housekeeper for a while now. It's not presentable inside."

Or there's something in there you don't want us to see, Allison thought. Taking a seat in a rocker sporting peeling wicker, Allison examined her host. "I was under the impression that you and Frank are about the same age, Mr. McIntosh. If I didn't have that bit of information, I'd find it hard to peg your age." Allison planted an innocent smile on her face. "Just how old are you, Mr. McIntosh?"

The twitch that marred McIntosh's mouth was so faint that had she not been looking for a reaction to her question, Allison would have missed the tell. "I'm a few years younger than Frankie here, and he's aged badly." McIntosh laughed.

Allison's expression never changed. More than a decade of trial work had ingrained in her the ability to hold a poker face, even when presented with testimony or evidence she knew to be false. And a false statement is exactly what Allison had just heard. Sean McIntosh had told Sheriff Trowbridge that he and Frank were the same age. Why would McIntosh lie about that?

"You told Sheriff Trowbridge you moved to Scotland when we were seven or eight," Frank interjected before Allison could stop him. "The operative word being 'we,'" Frank added, giving his cousin a suspicious look.

McIntosh shook his head. "No, the sheriff must have misheard me. I told him I moved to Scotland when you were seven or eight. My age isn't important," he added, dismissing the issue of his age with a wave of his hand. "What *is* important is finding Blue Scarlet. That's why you're here, isn't it? Ye've come to help me find Blue Scarlet?"

"I don't remember ever talking to you about a horse called Blue Scarlet. I don't remember taking your case. In fact, I don't remember ever talking to you at all. Not recently, not ever," Frank replied. "But I've got an open file on your case, and when Toby called you to tell you I'd been shot, you freaked out. I want to know why about a lot of things. Let's start with the horse you claim was stolen."

Sean McIntosh remained leaning against the porch rail where he had deposited his compact frame. Tamping once again his unlit pipe, McIntosh ignored Frank's question, seeming, perhaps, to be weighing his answer. With a brisk movement, McIntosh knocked the bowl of his pipe against the white porch railing, spilling unlit, smoked tobacco onto the porch's faded blue floor. Ignoring the mess and potential stain from the spilled tobacco, McIntosh raised his head. To Allison's and Frank's surprise, tears had filled the man's eyes. "She's a beauty, she is, my Blue Scarlet. Good lineage, sweet temperament for a race horse. I bought her to breed with Demon. Figured I'd have a Derby winner for sure out of that match." McIntosh pulled a worn leather pouch from his hip pocket, paused to refill his pipe with fresh tobacco, then used the blunt end of his knife to compact the tobacco to its proper density. "Five weeks ago, I left for a short trip to Miami. When I came back, Blue Scarlet was gone." McIntosh struck a match, held it over the bowl of the pipe, and puffed to ignite the tobacco. The pungent smell of cherry floated over Allison, causing a fleeting memory of her father to intrude. "Happened the night before I got back. Someone got in, got my girl out without a person here on the farm being aware. Had to be someone Blue Scarlet knew. Sweet temperament or not, she'd never have gone with a stranger without making a racket."

Allison digested the information she'd just heard. Discerning the truth was another talent Allison had developed as a result of her trial practice. Other than the weird twitch McIntosh had given when she questioned his age, Allison believed the man was telling the truth about Blue Scarlet. "You told

Sheriff Trowbridge that Blue Scarlet was insured but that the insurance company had no record of her."

"That's right, lassie." Sean nodded in agreement. "When the insurance company pulled my file, they said Blue Scarlet wasn't listed on the policy. But I know I insured her. I had the canceled check to prove I'd paid the premium. Those cretins at the insurance company said it didn't matter—if she wasn't named on the policy, she wasn't insured."

"I've handled my share of insurance claims," Allison told McIntosh. "The company's position seems a bit off to me. If you had proof of paying the premium, there should be coverage."

McIntosh fidgeted with his pipe. Allison remembered that pipes didn't stay lit for very long. "I argued with the agent for several days, even talked to a supervisor. Finally, the company said since I'd proved I'd paid the premium, if I could produce proof of ownership that they would pay the claim. That's when the real problem started."

"There's no record you ever bought that horse, am I right?" Frank remembered the notation Toby had recorded.

"Not only that, there's no record of Blue Scarlet ever existing," McIntosh replied.

"How is that possible?" Allison asked. "Where did you buy her? Wouldn't whoever you bought her from have a record of her birth?"

"I bought her at a small sale down in Clearwater. Hadn't heard of it before, just saw a small ad in the local paper. In retrospect, I should have wondered about the whole deal, but her papers looked legit and the blood line was stellar. Plus, the price was right," McIntosh explained. "First thing I tried to do was track down the guy who sold Blue Scarlet to me. He was a ghost."

What a tale, Allison thought and was surprised to find she felt sorry for Sean McIntosh. "I hate to say it, but I think you've been the victim of a scam, Mr. McIntosh."

"I agree," Frank added. "Someone who maybe knew your reputation figured you for a good mark."

Sean McIntosh laid his pipe on the porch railing. "Blasted pipe," Sean cussed. Putting his hands in his pockets, he shrugged. "That's my read on this, too. I just can't figure who would have been smart enough to do this to me."

"The question," Allison replied, "is not who was smart enough to do this to you. The first question is who would have a reason to do this to you. Setting you up for that initial purchase, leaving the horse with you for a year before stealing her, destroying any evidence of ownership—that took careful and extensive planning and more importantly, a strong desire to hurt you." Allison looked McIntosh in the eye. "Who have you hurt, Mr.

McIntosh? Who hates you badly enough to plan and execute a long con?"

"And why did you think that whoever shot me was coming after you?" Frank questioned.

Sean McIntosh scuffed the toe of his boot against the pile of used tobacco he had earlier tossed on the porch floor. "I haven't told you all of it."

"Which is?" Frank demanded. "What do you know about why I got shot?"

Sean McIntosh's lips tightened. The twitch appeared again in his cheek, but this time, Allison read the physical signs as a struggle to pass unsavory words. "I got a call. A man. Said he had information about Blue Scarlet, but it would cost me. Threatened me, actually—said if I contacted the authorities, it'd be the last call I ever made. I didn't know what to do, then I remembered I'd heard about you, that you were a private dick. I called you, told you about Blue Scarlet, told you about the call." Sadness filled Sean's eyes. "You went to the rendezvous instead of me. You almost got killed because of me."

Allison watched Frank's startled expression. "Do you remember any of this, Frank? Does any of what Sean is telling you seem familiar?"

Frank struggled against the fog that still clouded his memory. "No," he replied, "not a damn thing."

Turning her attention back to Sean McIntosh, Allison asked, "Have you been contacted again?"

The seriousness of McIntosh's demeanor answered Allison's question before his words did. "I thought he'd given up when I didn't hear anything after Frank was shot. I was wrong. Found this when I stepped outside this morning." Sean handed Allison a piece of crumpled paper. "It was pushed up under the front door of the house."

The handwriting appeared childish and unlettered, but its meaning was apparent: *Tol you no cops. The horse is dead. Yur next.*

CHAPTER FIFTEEN

Six Months Ago

"*B*astardo," Maria Sanchez wept as she cursed. "*Vete al diablo.*" The dark-haired woman jerked her arm from her tormentor's grip. "I won't do this," she declared defiantly.

"Don't be ridiculous, darlin'. Of course you will. You'll do everything I tell you, when I tell you, and without complaint," Plato McCall laughed. "Besides, what's it to you? Sean McIntosh cares nothing for you. You're just the hired help."

Maria shook her head, eyes flashing at the insult. "Senor McIntosh is a good man. He is kind to me."

Plato McCall threw a disdainful glance at his surroundings. Maria Sanchez's bodega, closed now for the evening, was illuminated by a sole lightbulb hanging from a cord in the middle of the small building's ceiling. An old, wooden counter made an L at the back and left side of the store, four short rows of merchandise tables filled the remaining space. Signs of a dirt floor peeped through portions of peeling linoleum, while three windows provided light during the daytime hours. But despite its age and wear, Maria Sanchez's bodega was pristinely clean.

"How'd you get this place, Maria?" Plato asked contemptuously.

"Senor McIntosh gave it to me," Maria whispered.

"How many times did you have to fuck him?" Plato's question was cruel. "That's how you paid for it isn't it, Maria?" Plato moved toward the woman. "You're just a whore, Maria. Just a piece of Mexican trash. Pussy's the only currency women like you have."

Fresh tears flowed from the distraught woman's eyes. "Why do you say these things to me?" she cried. "I have not slept with Senor McIntosh. He is simply kind to me, nothing more."

Fine leather boots encased Plato McCall's feet. Planting his right foot against the wooden counter, Plato withdrew a narrow, silver stiletto. "It's a fine example of workmanship, don't you think?" he asked. "Sharp as razor wire, deadly, too," he added, pointing the knife at Maria. "I can gut an animal in under a minute. Just think what I could do to a child."

"You would not." Maria gasped.

"Oh yes, my darlin', I would and I will if you don't do exactly as I say," Plato assured the woman. "I know where she is."

The sound of weeping increased. Maria Sanchez crumpled to the floor. "What is it I must do?" she asked the devil.

CHAPTER SIXTEEN

Present Day

When Allison and Jim bought ponies for Charlotte and Mack, the last thing they had imagined was that one of their children would become so enamored of the four-legged creatures that winning an Olympic medal would become her aspiration. But that was what had happened and was why Allison and Jim were sitting in the stands at the Western North Carolina Agricultural Center outside Asheville, North Carolina, getting ready to watch Charlotte and Diamond Girl compete in the junior dressage event.

Allison had learned a lot about equestrian sports over the past few years. Prior to engaging the services of Marion Hutcheson at Overlook Riding Club, all Allison knew about competitive riding was what she had gleaned from watching the events on TV every four years during the summer Olympic games. Now, Allison knew equestrian disciplines ranged from Western dressage to Paso Fino shows to hunter/jumper classes to English dressage, just to name a few. Competitions were held worldwide, ranging from small local events to those at the international levels. Shows could run anywhere from one to three days depending on the various performances, or classes, of competition. The event Charlotte was competing in today was a junior English dressage event, restricted to riders age fifteen and under. It was Charlotte's first foray into the big time.

"I don't know if my nerves can stand this," Allison moaned. "Marion swore Charlotte was ready for this event, but looking at the list of competitors, I'm not so sure."

Jim Kaufman gave his anxious wife a comforting pat. "Take a deep breath, babe. In fact, take a couple. Look at Charlotte. That child's made of ice when it comes to competitions—just like her mother during a trial. She'll be just fine."

Allison observed her oldest. Tan jodhpurs tucked neatly into shiny black riding boots; white shirt pressed to perfection peeping from a fitted riding jacket; a long, blond french braid escaping from the riding helmet intended to protect the rider from a fall, Charlotte Parker-Kaufman looked every inch the accomplished equestrian that Allison knew her child had become. Someday, if the fates smiled upon her daughter, Allison would recall this first competition as her child received an Olympic medal.

"You're right, of course." Allison smiled at her husband. "I always worried that Charlotte would be interested in gymnastics given her size. And to think, I thought flipping around the uneven bars or on the balance beam was dangerous."

The loud speaker broadcast Charlotte's name, drawing Allison's attention away from her husband and toward the exhibition ring. Charlotte's event was being held in the smaller of the two competition arenas, just 66 by 131 feet. Six judges were situated around the arena in order to view and score the horse and rider from different positions and angles. Scored individually, and not against other competitors in the class, Charlotte would receive anywhere from a zero for an unexecuted move to a ten for a perfect one.

Charlotte's time in the arena lasted less than five minutes. Taking a horse through the dressage moves did not take long; hours and hours of training were condensed into just a few minutes where the rider's skill, ability, appearance, and performance would be scored.

"The judges' score for Charlotte Parker-Kaufman and Diamond Girl is four point eight," the loud-speaker announced to the crowd.

Allison pumped a fist in the air with an accompanying "Yes!" Marion Hutcheson had told Allison before the competition that any score over a four on a rider's initial competition would be icing on the cake. What an exciting debut for Charlotte.

"See? I told you she'd be fine." Jim gave his wife a kiss on the cheek. "Let's head on down to the paddock and give our girl a big hug."

Taking her husband's offered hand for an assist down the narrow bleachers, Allison knew she had more than Charlotte's safe performance to be grateful for. On their way out of town for this event, Jim had received a call from Larry Fuller telling him the results of the nuclear stress test he had taken the week before. "Everything looks good, Jim," the doctor had reported. "Not sure why the EKG looked off, but the NST is a much more thorough test, and you passed with flying colors. Stick to your diet and exercise, and I'll see you in a year." Squeezing Jim's hand, Allison told her husband, "I love you."

"I love you, too, babe," Jim replied automatically, then noticing Allison's expression, stopped to ask, "Is everything all right?"

"Can't a wife tell her hunk of a husband that she loves him?" Allison brought a light tone to her reply. "I was just thinking how grateful I am—for you, for our children—and I wanted to express it."

"Keep that thought." Jim grinned. "I'll remind you of it tonight after the kids are in bed."

Before Allison could think of an appropriately salacious reply, she was nearly knocked to the ground by an exuberant Charlotte. "I did it!" squealed the young girl. "I really did it!"

"Yes, she did," agreed the tall woman following behind Charlotte, "but she still has lots of hard work ahead of her." Ruffling the child's hair, now freed from the black riding helmet, Marion Hutcheson remarked, "Enjoy your day, Charlotte. We'll be back at work on Monday. If you've got a minute," Marion directed her next words to Allison, "Jeri wanted me to let you know about a conversation she had with a trainer in Florida about Sean McIntosh."

So much time had passed since her conversation with Jeri Kennedy and Jeri's promise to see what she could find out about Sean McIntosh that following up with Jeri had slipped Allison's mind. Silently berating herself for her uncustomary forgetfulness, Allison responded, "I actually met Sean McIntosh a few days ago. Frank Martin and I went down to McIntosh's farm in north Florida. I'd be interested to hear what Jeri found out, see if it jibes with what Frank and I concluded after talking to the guy."

"Jeri called several of her old Florida contacts. She had about given up when she hit pay dirt with Joanie Teller. Joanie runs a big spread near Ocala. Her ear is as near to the ground as possible in the horse business." Marion paused to allow several people to pass by. When assured again of privacy, she continued. "Joanie had heard of McIntosh Farms but didn't really know much about its owner."

"So Jeri spent her time calling around for nothing?" Allison presumed. "I'm sorry she wasted her time on my account."

"Hold on, Allison, not so fast," Marion cautioned. "Joanie gave Jeri the name of a guy she'd grown up with in Boston named Plato McCall. Joanie said if there was anything to know about Sean McIntosh that Plato ought to know it."

Allison laughed. "What a name—Plato McCall. Whoever named him must have been a fan of the classics. Did Jeri get 'hold of him?"

"She left a message. Hasn't heard back. Thought you might want to call him yourself," Marion replied, handing Allison a folded piece of paper. "That's got his phone number, the address of his ranch, and also Joanie Teller's number. Jeri said for you just to call Joanie direct if you had any other questions. She gave Joanie your name, so you'd be familiar if you called."

"Tell Jeri I owe her," Allison requested. "I'll track this Plato guy down next week and see what he can tell me about Sean McIntosh." *It's always good to get a second or third opinion,* Allison thought as she and her family took their departure from Charlotte's coach. There was something off about Sean McIntosh's story, as believable as it was to her. He had told Allison the truth, she thought, just not the whole truth.

CHAPTER SEVENTEEN

Summers in Alabama weren't for the faint of heart. With humidity in the ninetieth percentile and temps often hanging near the hundred-degree mark for days or weeks, Frank Martin didn't think hell could be much worse. On this particular summer day, however, Frank was feeling heat of a different sort, and even though the sensation was nothing new to someone in his line of work, twenty-five years in the business had never acclimated the private investigator to testifying in open court about the details of a husband's or wife's infidelity.

Miles and Evelyn Goodpasture had been married for thirty years. Everyone in Fort Charles who knew the couple thought Miles and Evelyn were a strange pair, not because either was particularly weird, but rather, because they were so totally different from each other. Miles Goodpasture was outgoing, charismatic, and devilishly handsome. The adage that men aged much better than women had been borne out in the Goodpasture marriage. At the age of fifty-five, Miles Goodpasture worked out every day, ran a couple of half marathons each year, still wore thirty-four-inch-waist pants, and had such an unlined face that some suspicioned Miles had taken a trip to a popular cosmetic surgeon in Birmingham.

Evelyn, on the other hand, could have been Miles's maiden aunt. She wasn't fat, exactly, but the extra pounds Evelyn carried had accumulated over the years in direct proportion to Evelyn's lack of resistance to cookies, cakes, pies, and other sweets coupled with her outright refusal to darken the doors of the Fort Charles Athletic Club. People in general bored Evelyn. She preferred to spend her days reading about literary characters, which were much more interesting than the inhabitants of Fort Charles, Alabama. Disdaining any attempt to ameliorate the aging process and caring little for her appearance, Evelyn Goodpasture wore her steel-gray hair in a tight bun above a face that had never seen an ounce of makeup.

A couple of years back, gossip in the small Southern town had paired Miles with a new, young schoolteacher who had joined the faculty at Fort Charles Elementary. Before that, talk around town had the man being a member of a swinger's club supposedly located in Mobile. Miles's interest in anything good looking and female was well known. His tendency to attend parties and events without his wife added fuel to the fire of randy tales that periodically roared into life in the Goodpastures' social circle. Problem was, no one had ever caught Miles in any inappropriate circumstance. Flirting— and that was all that anyone had ever been able to substantiate—well, flirting wasn't illegal.

Frank had tried to dissuade Miles Goodpasture from wasting his money when he first came to Frank's office. "I've been doing PI work for a long time, Mr. Goodpasture. I've got a pretty good nose for the sort of extramarital activity you think your wife is engaged in. Based on everything I know about Mrs. Goodpasture, I just can't see it," Frank had explained. "But it's your money. I'll spend a few days tailing your wife and then let you know if I uncover anything."

Boy, had Frank been wrong about Evelyn Goodpasture. And now, he'd been subpoenaed by Miles Goodpasture's attorney to testify in the couple's divorce trial. At least the case was in Judge

Kaufman's court. Neither side would be permitted to engage in shenanigans. The judge ran a tight ship.

"State your name for the record," Taylor Kitchens, Miles's attorney ordered Frank.

"Frank Martin."

"What is your occupation, Mr. Martin?"

"I'm a private investigator. Been licensed in Alabama since 1991."

"Were your services retained by the plaintiff, Miles Goodpasture?"

"Yes." Frank nodded. "Mr. Goodpasture hired me about a year ago."

"What did Mr. Goodpasture hire you to do?" Taylor Kitchens smiled. One of Fort Charles's best divorce attorneys, Taylor enjoyed going for the jugular. The witness's upcoming answer was the first nail the attorney intended to drive in Evelyn Goodpasture's figurative coffin.

"Mr. Goodpasture believed that his wife was having an affair. He engaged me to find evidence of such if he was, in fact, correct about his wife's behavior." Frank shifted uncomfortably on the hard, cushionless wooden chair inside the witness box. The courtroom was packed with curious onlookers. Scanning the crowd, Frank recognized more than a few of the town's social elite. *Like sharks circling a wounded comrade*, Frank thought.

"And did you find such evidence?"

Taylor's question was quickly interrupted by Evelyn's attorney, Mark Lockridge. "Objection. Calls for a legal conclusion."

"Sustained," Judge Kaufman ruled. "Rephrase your question, Counselor," he instructed.

"What, if anything, did you discover about Mrs. Goodpasture's activities?" Kitchens asked Frank.

Taking a deep breath, Frank cleared his throat and offered Kitchens an opening salvo. "I discovered that Mrs. Goodpasture was having sexual relations with a man other than her husband."

Kitchens busied himself with several sheets of paper lying on the podium before him, seemingly searching for something he had mislaid. Frank knew better. Miles Goodpasture's attorney was whetting the appetite of the courtroom audience, building up suspense before his next question. "Were you able to discern the identity of Mrs. Goodpasture's paramour?" Kitchens asked quietly.

"Yes." Frank stopped. He'd make Kitchens ask the necessary follow-up question.

"Who was Mrs. Goodpasture having sex with?" Kitchens pushed.

"Pierre Chastain," Frank replied.

A collective gasp of disbelief escaped from the spectators' gallery. Pierre Chastain was one of Fort Charles's most eligible bachelors. Furthermore, he was at least ten years younger than Evelyn Goodpasture.

"Was Mr. Chastain the only person with whom Mrs. Goodpasture was having sexual relations?" Kitchens struggled to suppress a smile. He never asked a question for which he didn't already know the answer.

"No." Frank's reply was curt.

"How many persons did you observe Evelyn Goodpasture having sexual relations with, Mr. Martin?" Kitchens pressed.

Frank hesitated. He had always liked Evelyn Goodpasture, had felt sorry for her being married to a narcissist like Miles. The testimony he was being compelled to give would ruin Evelyn—not socially, though. Frank knew Evelyn could care less what people thought about her. No, this testimony exposing Evelyn's passion and secret life would ruin her at the very core of her being. Adultery or not, Frank felt sympathy for Evelyn Goodpasture. "There were three others," Frank replied softly.

In response to Kitchen's questioning, Frank informed Judge Kaufman—divorce proceedings were never decided by a jury—that he had filmed Evelyn Goodpasture in various acts of sexual intercourse, some of which were still illegal in the state of Alabama, with two other men and one woman. When Kitchens made known his intent to show Frank's films in open court and to introduce them as evidence, a brief battle ensued between counsels for the parties over the admissibility of Frank's work. After questioning Frank about chain of custody and other pertinent issues, Judge Kaufman ruled in favor of Miles Goodpasture. The courtroom's inhabitants sat transfixed for the next forty-five minutes watching Evelyn Goodpasture's performance. By the time Kitchens advised, "I tender the witness," for Frank's cross-examination, Evelyn Goodpasture was weeping quietly.

Mark Lockridge was as good an attorney as his opponent, but the testimony and recorded evidence from Frank posed an insurmountable obstacle in his defense of Evelyn Goodpasture. Mark scored points where he could, attacking Frank's memory, calling into question some of Frank's methods, but in the end, he had made no real dent in Frank's testimony. An hour after he began his cross-examination, Lockridge advised Judge Kaufman that he was finished with the witness.

Wisely, Kitchens had declined any redirect of Frank. Frank's testimony was intact, and more importantly, the films of Evelyn's transgressions were in evidence. Standing at counsel table, Kitchens told Judge Kaufman, "We have no further questions for this witness, Your Honor."

The large clock on the back wall of Judge Kaufman's courtroom showed 2:45 p.m. as Frank walked under it and pushed open the double doors that allowed his departure from the courtroom. Frank wasn't much of a drinker, but today's experience had left him feeling dirty and sad. On his way back to the office, Frank detoured into the ABC Store on Main Street. Frank and Johnny Walker had a date for the rest of the afternoon.

CHAPTER EIGHTEEN

Five Years Ago

Maria Camila Luciana Sanchez had been born into a life of wealth and privilege thanks to the rapacious and adventurous nature of Alfonse Sanchez, the patriarch of the Sanchez clan, who had immigrated to Chile during the Spanish colonization of that country in the late seventeen hundreds. By the time Maria was born in her mother's bedroom in the palatial Sanchez hacienda, the Sanchez family had become outrageously wealthy. Owning thousands of acres of land overlying rich copper deposits, Maria Sanchez's family had used the natural resource to survive Chile's torrid history of political upheaval and economic difficulties. Democracy of a sort may have emerged in Chile in the mid-nineteen hundreds, but families like Maria's continued to enjoy a lifestyle more reminiscent of the landed gentry of earlier centuries.

The life of restriction and obedience to tradition had chafed at Maria. Allowed no friends outside her family's narrow and rarified circle of wealthy compatriots, Maria yearned for the life she glimpsed on the few occasions she traveled to Valparaíso or Viña del Mar with her mother and sisters.

"Mama, please," Maria begged on the eve of her seventeenth birthday. "Can't I go to the university next year?"

"What are you thinking?" her mother had reprimanded. "Your life is here, with your own kind. Besides, your father and I have selected a husband for you. Forget your foolish ideas about the university."

The summer of her seventeenth year had passed quickly. Spending hours each day riding her Paso Fino across the verdant fields of the Sanchez estate, Maria began to plan. She would not be married off to some man she had never seen, someone she did not know, much less someone she did not love. If her parents attempted to force such a marriage on her, Maria needed to be able to escape.

Where she had found the courage to actually leave her home and all she knew would be a question

Maria would ask herself for the remainder of her life. Taking only what she could fit in a small backpack that she had earlier concealed in her horse's stall, Maria arose before dawn on the day she was to meet her betrothed, rode her beloved horse to near exhaustion before turning him loose to be found later by one of the Sanchez ranch hands, and then hitched a ride on a produce truck headed to Valparaíso.

The small hotel Maria found was seedy, but the girl knew she had to conserve the meager amount of money she had been able to save for her escape, and she was afraid her parents would search for her in the nicer hotels in the city. Plus, Maria wasn't sure how much she would have to pay to be smuggled onto a boat in Valparaíso's port. If she needed more, maybe one of the pieces of her mother's jewelry that she had purloined would make up the difference. Although not wise in the ways of the larger world, Maria knew instinctively to guard the existence of the jewels she had brought with her.

Later, Maria realized she must have been an obvious mark to the old woman running the hotel where Maria had paid her few pesos for an overnight accommodation. Desperate and afraid of being caught by her father, Maria had foolishly confided her dilemma to the innkeeper. "Capitan Morso will take you to America," the woman told Maria. "It will cost you, though. Twenty-eight thousand pesos."

"I don't have that much," Maria replied. "Will the *capitan* let me work off my fare?" she asked innocently.

The old woman smiled. "I'm sure you can work something out with Capitan Morso. He is a reasonable man."

The old woman had been only partially right. The captain did, indeed, allow Maria to work off the cost of her fare. Reasonable, however, was not a word that would ever be used to describe Capitan Franco Morso. Ten days after she set sail on Capitan Morso's ship, Maria Sanchez arrived on the west coast of Florida a victim of repeated rape at the hands of the man she had thought to be her savior. Bleeding and bruised, Maria had stumbled from the beach where Morso had dumped her and her meager belongings, then crawled toward the faint sound of cars she heard in the distance. "*Jesus, Hijo de Dios*," she prayed, the words barely passing her cut lips. "*Salvame, por favor. Salvame.*"

The scratch of rough pavement on her hands and knees registered faintly in a far-off part of Maria's brain as she pulled her body from the high grass onto the blacktop of a two-lane highway. Dimly, she was aware of a white light that was getting brighter and brighter, approaching at a rapid pace. Maybe it was the Archangel Michael, she thought, sent to answer her prayers.

"Mother of God," Maria heard a male voice exclaim.

Squinting through swollen eyes, Maria raised her head. The glare of a car's headlights enveloped the figure of a man, now kneeling and touching Maria with gentle hands, endowing him with an angelic aura. "Archangel?" she whispered.

"There's no angels around here, lassie," the man told Maria, "although come to think of it, I don't usually take this road home." A small moan escaped Maria as the man gently lifted her from the pavement and cradled her against his body. "Don't you worry, lassie. I'll have you to the hospital faster than a Leprechaun's magic."

Sean McIntosh watched the needle on his truck's speedometer pass eighty-five. He figured the woman lying in the back seat of his F-450 had about a fifty-fifty chance of survival. If she lived, he'd do what he could to help her.

CHAPTER NINETEEN

Present Day

Depositions in the Allied Plastics case had consumed most of Allison's week. Unable to schedule the discovery matters for Fort Charles, Allison and her opposing counsel had agreed to a neutral location at a Birmingham law firm. This week, Allison had deposed the plaintiff and several of his witnesses, while Matt Aiken had harassed and hammered at the CEO of Allied Plastics with questions irrelevant to the merits of the plaintiff's case but that were obviously intended to provoke and irritate Allison's client. Allison had entered numerous objections to the questions "on the record" ensuring that her objections would be preserved in the transcript the court reporter was recording. Questioning in discovery depositions was pretty much wide open. Most courts, including the federal court in Birmingham where the case would be tried, allowed attorneys great leeway during depositions, ruling on the appropriateness and admissibility of the question and answer later at trial.

Allison hated to travel for business and tried to avoid it unless there was absolutely no way to avoid it. Being home with Charlotte and Mack each evening was important to her. This week, adding a four-hour round-trip commute each day to the long hours of depositions had been exhausting. When the last deposition concluded after seven last night, Allison had fortified herself with a double espresso from the Starbucks drive-through before heading back to Fort Charles. This morning, examining the stack of correspondence, court notices, and phone messages Donna had left on her desk, Allison pushed the lingering fatigue from her mind.

Returning phone calls was always Allison's first priority. A client, whether established or prospective, deserved and expected a timely response. Allison had never forgotten an article in the *Alabama Bar Magazine* about client complaints. The number one offender was the delay in returning the client's phone calls. Calls that came for Allison were returned by the end of the workday if at all possible. During extended periods out of the office, the caller was informed there would be a delay in Allison returning the call, and the caller would be offered an opportunity to speak with David Jackson if the matter was urgent and the caller did not want to wait until Allison returned. Allison did the same for David with the result that along with a reputation for excellent legal work, Parker & Jackson maintained a high client-satisfaction rating.

Picking up the thin stack of pink phone messages—Allison still liked the old-fashioned method of taking down calls rather than electronic messaging—she returned the calls in the order they were received, touching base with those who had called at the beginning of her week away and ending with the ones received yesterday afternoon. Forty-five minutes after she began returning calls, answering client questions, setting up appointments, and otherwise reassuring various high-maintenance clients that all was well with their respective legal matters, Allison reached the last pink phone slip.

In neat handwriting, Donna Pevey had written, "Plato McCall. Said he was returning your call. Gave me two numbers to pass on to you. What case is this? I don't recall that name." Allison smiled. Her secretary liked to be one step ahead of her boss when it came to clients, their names, contact information, and case data. Allison had not yet shared any information about Plato McCall with Donna. Picking up the receiver of her desk phone, Allison rang her secretary's extension.

"Donna, did Plato McCall say anything to you when he called for me?"

"No," her secretary answered, "and who in the daylights is Plato McCall? Have I missed a new client?"

"He's not a client," Allison rushed to assure Donna. "You're still on the top of your game. You haven't missed a thing. I'm hoping Mr. McCall will be a source of information about Sean McIntosh, the guy who hired Frank and then almost got him killed."

Mollified, Donna offered her boss everything she could remember about the call. "He asked for you. Said he was returning your call. I told him you were out of town in depositions, probably for most of the week, and asked if he'd like to talk to Mr. Jackson. Now that I think back on it, the guy did seem kind of irritated that you weren't here to take his call—made some comment about wasting his time or how valuable his time was, something like that." Donna paused, and Allison heard the soft clicking of her secretary's keyboard in the background. "Yep, here it is," Donna continued. "I made a note about him because the name wasn't familiar and because he was really rude to me. After he complained about his time being wasted or whatever, he gave me his numbers and then hung up on me. Not so much as a 'kiss my ass' either." Donna's softly muttered "Jerk" summarized her feelings about Mr. Plato McCall.

Before Allison could interrogate her secretary further, Donna's quick, "Got a call coming in," cut short further discussion. Pondering Donna's recap of her conversation with Plato McCall, Allison considered her secretary's take on the man versus the information she had received from Jeri Kennedy. Donna Pevey had an uncanny ability when it came to assessing people. A few minutes on a phone call wasn't much time to get a read on someone, but Donna's batting average was in the .500s. Being a rude jerk on the phone wasn't a terrible character defect, but the fact that Plato McCall had rubbed Donna the wrong way was a fact Allison would not forget.

Typing a command, Allison pulled up the copy of the Martin Investigation file on Sean McIntosh and McIntosh Farms that she had scanned into her computer the week before. A quick click of the mouse revealed a drop-down menu with several sub-files Allison had created. Moving the mouse to the third file listed, Allison placed the cursor on the title "Plato McCall" and reviewed what she had on the man.

Jeri Kennedy had been true to her word. After speaking with Joanie Teller, Jeri had tracked down Plato McCall at his horse farm near Gainsville. According to Jeri, Plato McCall was from Boston, had inherited a good bit of money, and made more money in the horse business. "Joanie said she hadn't seen McCall since high school until about a year ago when he bought his ranch," Jeri had related to Allison. "Still, Joanie said she's always thought McCall was a good guy, and he'd probably be willing to help you if he could."

Sitting back in her desk chair, Allison thought about the discrepancy in Jeri's description of Plato McCall and the gut assessment her secretary had made. Jeri's report reflected opinions of the man's peers—people Plato McCall did business with and/ or with whom he might socialize. Donna's contact with the man had been on a completely different basis. In that instance, Plato McCall had been addressing, or dressing down, a secretary. Allison had her own opinion of people whose treatment of others was based solely on social- or working-class status. A frown marred her attractive features as Allison assigned Plato McCall to a drawer in her mental file cabinet reserved for snobs, egotists, and narcissists.

The grandfather clock in the firm's reception area sounded noon and reminded Allison that her six o'clock chocolate SlimFast breakfast shake had quit doing its job of keeping her full, no matter how many grams of protein it had. Maybe she could grab Frank for a quick lunch. One quick call and ten minutes later, Allison and Frank had settled into a booth at Doe's Diner.

"I know I shouldn't order that pimento cheese burger," Allison lamented, "but I just can't resist. Why did I ever let you talk me into eating here today?"

"You eat like a damn bird," Frank retorted. "Ain't healthy."

"And you need to eat more like a bird unless you want to end up back in the hospital," Allison quickly replied. "You know what Dr. Lopez said about you losing weight."

"Harrumph," Frank groused, throwing down the menu in disgust. "If you're going to eat that cheeseburger, you can't do it in front of me. That's downright mean."

"How about a compromise?" Allison asked. "Chicken salad on whole wheat. Fruit instead of chips. Think you can live with that?"

Frank gave a reluctant nod. "Could be worse," he reflected.

Waiting for their order Allison shared her thoughts about Plato McCall with the investigator. "I've got two people whose opinions I value giving me two completely different assessments about the same person. Jeri's relying on what a third party has told her about McCall and that sort of information is always a little suspect. Donna, on the other hand, actually spoke with him, and her read on the man wasn't very good. Given the circumstances, I'm inclined to go with Donna's assessment."

"Thanks, Dianne." Frank smiled as the waitress deposited an extralarge sandwich in front of him. Taking an enormous bite out of the overflowing offering, Frank reflected on Allison's statement. "I agree," he replied, washing down half of his sandwich with a glass of sweet tea. "I don't know Joanie Teller, and that's who Jeri Kennedy is relying on for her information."

"That's my thinking, too." Allison reluctantly scraped the chicken salad from the bread, discarding the unneeded carbs. "But we need more information about Plato McCall than what we have."

A loud belch announced the end of Frank's repast. "Sorry 'bout that," Frank apologized, wiping his mouth with a paper napkin. "My stomach still isn't used to real food yet."

Allison laughed her reply. "Frank Martin, there's nothing new about you burping. Losing part of your stomach is no excuse."

Ignoring the gentle reprimand, Frank returned to the lunchtime topic. "We do need more information on McCall, and I'm going to get it." Seeing the alarm in Allison's eyes, Frank raised his hand. "Wait.

I'm not finished. I realize McCall may be the man who shot me. No sense in coming at the guy straight ahead." Frank motioned the waitress for a refill on his tea. "I want to nose around Sean's ranch for a few days. Talk to some of his ranch hands. See if anything clicks for me."

"You be careful, Frank," Allison cautioned. "I'm still not convinced Sean McIntosh is who he says is."

"I hear you." Frank nodded grimly. "Believe me, I'm not interested in getting shot again."

CHAPTER TWENTY

Cullman, Alabama, is a small, mostly white town of fewer than ten thousand souls nestled in the southernmost extension of the Appalachian Mountains. Founded in 1873 by a German refugee, Cullman solicited and welcomed large numbers of German immigrants to the area in the twenty years that followed its establishment. Many of the immigrants were adherents of the Lutheran Church, but an equally large number of immigrants were Catholic. Saint Bernard Abbey, founded in the 1840s, offered the monastic life to Catholic men, while Sacred Heart Monastery offered a cloistered life to Catholic women.

For a period of almost a hundred years, the monks of Saint Bernard Abbey operated a high school, a junior college, a four-year college, and a seminary. By the 1980s, however, the ministry of both Saint Bernard Abbey and Sacred Heart Monastery had expanded beyond institutional education to include hosting private or group retreats, days of reflection, and other events designed to meet the spiritual and educational needs of those seeking guidance as well as provide needed revenue for the abbey and monastery.

Setting aside a letter from Sister Angelina, the mother superior at Sacred Heart Monastery, Sean McIntosh reflected on the circumstances that had led him to seek the help of a church he had long since abandoned. Sean McIntosh's childhood and education had been permeated by the teachings of the "one true church." Daily mass, altar boy, member of the Catholic Youth Ministry—Sean McIntosh had spent the first fifteen years of his life believing the priesthood would be his path. When his mother was diagnosed with ovarian cancer, Sean was not concerned. His mother was a devout Catholic, so was his father. Sean knew exactly what would happen: Father Angus had assured him that God always answered the prayers of the faithful, and no one was more faithful than Sean McIntosh. God and his Son would intervene and heal his mother from the cancer that was devouring her.

Collete McIntosh died three months after her diagnosis. Deciding that either Father Angus had lied or the Almighty was a cruel ass, Sean had turned his back on the church in particular and religion in general. For more than forty years, Sean had dismissed the lessons of his childhood, castigating himself for believing nonsense, deriding himself for drinking the Kool-Aid. And life had been just fine until the headlights of his truck had illuminated the battered body of Maria Sanchez on that lonely highway five years earlier.

Picking up the letter from his desk, Sean read again the disturbing sentences of Sister Angelina's letter. *Isabella is a bright child. Her disability has not affected her mind, and she is a pleasure to have in our care. We have discussed, however, if whether it would be in the child's best interest to be sent elsewhere, to live in a community where she can have interaction with other children, and where she can perhaps receive better care as she becomes older. Sacred Heart is not an orphanage. This you knew when we agreed to shelter Isabella. If her mother cannot take the child back, then it is our recommendation that Isabella be moved elsewhere or perhaps placed for adoption.*

A deep sigh escaped Sean's lips. He had known this day would eventually come; he had just hoped it would not be this soon. The sun had barely reached its zenith, but ignoring the hour, Sean opened the small liquor cabinet in the corner of his office and poured a stiff shot of whiskey. The amber liquid burned slightly as it slipped past his tongue and down his throat. Sean paced, sipping his courage, reflecting on the past, wondering how or if he could have changed it.

That Maria Sanchez had been alive had been a miracle in itself. The emergency room doctor at the hospital in Gainesville told Sean he had never seen anyone beaten so severely survive. "She must have an extraordinary will to live," the doctor had remarked. "That and her youth are likely what have kept her alive." Strong will and youth notwithstanding, Maria's injuries had indeed been severe—a broken nose, hairline fracture of her jaw, bruised kidneys, multiple cuts and abrasions, internal bleeding—so severe that Maria had remained hospitalized for several weeks.

For reasons he had not understood, Sean McIntosh kept vigil over the young woman. Maybe it was pity, perhaps an unconscious memory of his mother's anguished end, but for whatever reason, by the time the doctors released Maria Sanchez from their care, Sean had prepared the guest suite at McIntosh Farms for Maria's continued recovery.

Pouring a refill from the half-empty fifth of Dewar's, Sean allowed the memories to flow.

Maria Sanchez had been six months along in her pregnancy before she realized she was carrying a child, the product of her repeated rape by the captain of the boat she had taken to escape her homeland. "Marry me," Sean had entreated, for during Maria's convalescence, he had fallen in love with her. "Marry me. I will care for you and your wee babe as if it were my own."

But Maria had refused. "This is not your burden," she had replied. "I have stayed here with you too long. When the child is born, I shall leave."

Isabella Valeria Sanchez was born on a crisp fall day. Her mother's labor had been easy with no indication that Isabella would arrive in the world less than whole. The doctor's whispered, "Oh," was the first clue that all had not been right. Sean swallowed the last of his drink remembering the shock of Isabella's condition. "Spina bifida with myeloschisis," the doctor had explained. "We can correct the cord protrusion, but the child will likely suffer some degree of paralysis. Only time will tell whether the paralysis is permanent."

Picking up the nun's letter for a second time, Sean wadded the missive in his fist. Isabella's paralysis had indeed been permanent. After the child's birth, Sean had urged Maria to contact her family. Surely, they would forgive Maria and help her provide a home for Isabella. "If you won't marry me, at least let your family help."

"You do not understand, Sean," Maria had replied. "I have brought disgrace to my family. There is no going back."

In the end, Sean had convinced Maria to place Isabella with the sisters at Sacred Heart Monastery in Cullman until she was able to care for her daughter herself. Thorough research and questions to the right people had provided Sean an entrée to the nuns. At three months of age, Isabella was welcomed into the care of the cloistered nuns. Accepting Sean's gift of the small bodega outside Bell, Maria had worked hard, saving every penny she could toward a day that might never come—the day she could provide a real home for her daughter.

Sean dialed the bodega.

"*¿Buenas noches. Cómo puedo ayudarte?*"

"It's me." Sean knew Maria would recognize his voice. "We need to talk."

Fear gripped Maria's heart. Had she been caught out? Did Sean McIntosh know what she had done? Worse yet, had the devil done something to her child? "Is it Isabella?" Maria could barely force the words across her tongue.

Sean heard the barely suppressed terror in Maria's question. "No, it's not Isabella," he began. "Well, it is, but she's not hurt or sick," he hurried to assure the child's mother. "But the news is not good.

I've received a letter from Sister Angelina. They cannot keep Isabella any longer. You must take her, or the nuns will press to allow her to be adopted."

For a moment, only silence answered Sean. "Maria? Are you still on the line?"

"*Sí.*" Maria Sanchez considered her options. Sean McIntosh had saved her life. He had found a refuge for her daughter and given her shelter. Sean McIntosh loved her. Of that Maria had no doubt. But was his love for her strong enough to withstand the truth—the truth of her betrayal? Maria did not think that possible of any man, even a man like Sean McIntosh. Still, she needed his help. "Can you help me, Sean?"

"You know I will," Sean's reply was quick and strong. "And this time, we're doing it my way. I'll contact the monastery and let them know we will be there this weekend to pick up Isabella. Take the rest of the week to close up the bodega and pack your belongings. You and Isabella are moving in with me—permanently."

Maria knew she should tell Sean about the devil and what she had done. But she could not. The instinct to protect her child was too strong. "*Gracias,* Sean," Maria whispered. *I'll tell him later,* she assured her conscience, *after Isabella is safe.* Maria ignored the voice in her head that answered, *Isabella will never be safe—not until Sean knows everything.*

CHAPTER TWENTY-ONE

Jim Kaufman loved the law. Hired into the Calhoun County District Attorney's office upon his graduation from law school, Jim Kaufman thought he would spend his career prosecuting criminals. American jurisprudence deemed the defendant innocent until proven otherwise. Jim believed this established tenet of the law without question, but he also believed in the concept of justice—justice for the perpetrator of a crime and justice for the victim. The small statue of Lady Justice, her eyes blindfolded, her arm holding aloft the scales of justice, a gift from his grandmother so many years ago, still graced the desk in his judicial chambers thirty years later.

Jim's election to the bench had surprised him. Encouraged by friends to run for the seat being vacated by a retiring and well-loved judge, Jim Kaufman had calculated his chance of election at less than 50 percent. After all, his opponent was an established trial lawyer whose family ties to Fort Charles and Calhoun County went back multiple generations. What Jim had not considered was the record his ten years as a prosecutor had provided. The voters of Calhoun County knew a fair-minded man when they saw one. Jim Kaufman had been elected with 60 percent of the vote. Reelection four years later saw his win margin increased by double percentage points. Twenty years later, the residents of Calhoun County continued to express their faith in Judge Jim Kaufman every election cycle.

As a circuit court judge, Jim Kaufman heard both civil and criminal cases. Civil cases ran the gamut of disputes, while any criminal matter regardless of whether a misdemeanor or a felony ended up in Jim's courtroom. Most judges, if being honest, will admit to enjoying some sorts of legal cases over others, and Jim Kaufman was no exception. Criminal cases could be disturbing, but Jim's ten years in the DA's office had inured him to most violent crime. The judge understood the horror associated with many criminal acts, as well as the impact on the victim of that crime, but he had long since been able to compartmentalize the acts from the application of the law.

No so with abuse cases involving children. As a parent, Jim's response to violence against children was guttural, instinctive, and if acted upon, would have a very bad ending for the perpetrator. As a judge, however, Jim had been forced to restrain his personal feelings in order to fairly apply the law. The phrase he had learned in law school—that the law was a strict task mistress—was no truer than in the fair application of state law to an accused child molester, rapist, or murderer.

A close second to criminal cases involving children, however, came nasty divorce cases. Fortunately for Jim, he rarely heard divorces. In Alabama, chancery courts had jurisdiction over divorces and child custody matters. Only rarely, and in the case of a conflict or recusal of the presiding judge, would Jim, as a circuit court judge, be asked to hear a domestic matter. In a small town like Fort Charles, it was difficult for a sitting judge not to know many of the litigants who might appear before him or her. Therefore, most motions asking that the judge recuse him-/herself because of familiarity with the parties would be denied. Only when the judge was actually a relative of one of the litigants would there be sufficient grounds for recusal. The sole chancery judge in Calhoun County happened to be Miles Goodpasture's uncle on his mother's side. Before Evelyn's lawyer had even filed a recusal motion, Judge Carson had removed himself from the Goodpasture divorce case and transferred it to Jim Kaufman's courtroom.

The evidence and testimony in the Goodpasture case had been damaging and one-sided. Courtrooms were open to the public, and unless being called as a witness, anyone who wanted to could attend a trial as an observer. Miles and Evelyn Goodpasture's so-called friends had packed the courtroom, eager to hear the dirt on their neighbors, ready to render their own judgment against people who had once been welcome guests in their homes.

Jim had spent the last hour reviewing the notes he made during the divorce proceedings. At his request, the judge's law clerk had prepared a summary of the elements required to prove Miles Goodpasture's legal claims. Jim reached for it now, more to assure himself that he had come to the right decision required by Alabama law, than to seek the answer that he already had.

Miles Goodpasture would be granted a divorce on the grounds of adultery. Contrary to popular belief, this did not mean that Evelyn Goodpasture would not receive alimony. Under Alabama law, Judge Kaufman was required to consider various factors: the earning ability of the spouses, the future prospects of the spouses, the length of the marriage, the standard of living of the spouses prior to the divorce, and whether the conduct of the spouses led to the divorce. Applying all of these factors, Alabama law then required the judge to make an "equitable" division of the divorcing couple's property and assets.

Evelyn was screwed. Jim admonished himself even as he acknowledged the unhappy truth of the thought that entered his mind. Evelyn had never worked. Now in her midfifties and with little in the way of marketable skills, Evelyn would be entitled to some amount of alimony even though she would be found guilty of adultery. It just wouldn't be much. Dictating the opinion to be typed for his signature, Jim wondered what sort of life Evelyn Goodpasture would have going forward. Regardless of whether she had brought this disaster on herself, Jim Kaufman felt sorry for the shell of a woman who had exited his courtroom at the end of trial. The judgment he was rendering would be inconsequential when compared to the judgment Fort Charles's society would impose on one of its own.

CHAPTER TWENTY-TWO

"There's too many freakin' buttons on this thing." Frustration seeped from Frank's voice as he tried to keep his new truck on the two-lane highway while figuring out how to turn up the country–blue grass mix pouring out of the Sony ten-speaker sound system that had come standard on his new Ford F-150. Allison's generosity with the Boudreaux settlement had included a substantial bonus tacked onto Frank's fee for the PI work he had done on that case.

Deciding a reward was in order, Frank had allowed himself to be sold the most-expensive and best-equipped truck on the lot at Ewing Ford in

Fort Charles. A 360-degree camera system, adaptive cruise control, quad beam LED headlights, remote tailgate release—all those technology features were great, Frank had to admit, but the feature that had sold Frank on his new ride were the multicontour massaging front seats. "You sure that's legal?" Frank had asked the car salesman after trying out the driver's seat's magic hands. "Never mind," Frank had interrupted the salesman's response. "I'll take her."

Assured that he had achieved the appropriate sound level for the new CD from the Steep Canyon Rangers, a group from Brevard, North Carolina, that Frank had discovered the year before, the private investigator turned his thoughts to the purpose of his trip. In the past two weeks since he and Allison had visited McIntosh Farms, Frank had spent as much of his free time as possible researching his cousin's backstory. It hadn't been easy. Frank's connections were all stateside. Getting information about Sean's years in Scotland on his own had been much more difficult than Frank had initially thought. Fortunately, Frank's FBI contact, Jake Cleveland, had put him in touch with an old Scotland Yard acquaintance. One thing Frank had learned over the years was that members of law enforcement would almost universally do anything possible to help one another. This unspoken rule of brotherhood had paid off once again.

To Frank's surprise, everything Sean McIntosh had said appeared true—at least as far as Sean's mother and stepfather, Sean's businesses in Scotland, his subsequent move to the States, and his establishment of McIntosh Farms in Bell, Florida. The veracity of Sean's story about Blue Scarlet, however, was yet to be determined and was the main reason Frank had decided to spend a few days in Bell. That plus a niggling feeling at the back of Frank's brain that Sean McIntosh was hiding something important about, and possibly relevant to, the alleged disappearance of the horse. Driving under the arched entry to McIntosh Farms, Frank was determined to dig deeper.

"What's yer poison, Frankie boy?" Sean McIntosh grinned at his cousin. "I've got me some fine malt whiskey. Brought it back with me last trip I made home."

Frank shook his head. "Nah, just a beer if you've got any. I try to stay away from the hard stuff 'cept for special occasions," he explained.

"And what is this if not a special occasion?" Sean asked. "Two cousins spending time together after being apart for forty years."

"Just a beer," Frank grunted. "This is business."

Sean reached into a small bar fridge and handed Frank a Budweiser. "Indeed it is," he replied, "and a nasty business at that. Have you had any luck the past couple of days?"

"I've spoken to every ranch hand you have. They all back your story about Blue Scarlet, but no one saw a thing the night she was taken. This morning, I drove into Gainesville and talked with your insurance agent." Frank upended the brown bottle, taking in the last sip of beer. "Got another?" he asked, tipping the empty toward his cousin.

Supplying Frank with a second libation, Sean pressed, "What did you find out? I told that guy to let you look at any of my policies and claims you wanted."

"Yeah," Frank acknowledged, "the agent was helpful. Without actually saying so, the guy admitted the insurance company probably dropped the ball with the paperwork insuring Blue Scarlet. You know that, otherwise the company would never have paid your claim."

"Don't see how they could have refused," Sean huffed. "I had the canceled check proving I had paid the premium."

"Agreed, but I don't think the issue with coverage has anything to do with Blue Scarlet's abduction," Frank concluded. "I think this is personal. And I think there's something you aren't telling me." Frank heaved himself from the leather club chair where he had been sitting. "It's been a long day and I'm tired. You got something else to tell me, be ready to talk in the morning."

Sean listened to Frank's footsteps tread heavily on the wooden stairs to the upstairs guest room. He didn't see how his relationship with Maria Sanchez was relevant to Frank's investigation, but that was the only thing Sean had not shared with his cousin. If Blue Scarlet's abduction was personal, then Sean had to ask himself who would want to hurt him and why? Beyond that currently unanswerable question came an equally troubling one: who had given the horse thief access to McIntosh Farms the night Blue Scarlet was taken? If Frank was correct, and no one working for McIntosh Farms was involved or had any knowledge of the abduction, who did that leave? Sean shifted uncomfortably in his chair, unwilling to admit that the woman he loved was the only person who fit that description.

Sean glanced at his watch. He had a few hours left to decide what, if anything, he would share with Frank at breakfast. Offering a silent plea for clarity to whatever Being might be listening, Sean followed Frank's lead and turned in for the night.

CHAPTER
TWENTY-THREE

"All rise," the bailiff demanded. Responding automatically, Allison rose to her feet as Judge Lee, the chief judge for the federal court for the Northern District of Alabama, entered the courtroom and took his seat on the bench overlooking the lawyers, litigants, jury, and spectators. Slim of build, with snow-white hair, Judge Percival Lee looked years younger than his sixty-five. "Be seated," the judge announced, allowing all in the courtroom to take their respective seats, waiting for the judge to continue.

Jury selection in Allison's Allied Plastics case had concluded late the day before. Eight members of the local community had been selected by Allison and opposing counsel, Matt Aiken, from a jury pool of several hundred: five women and three men, of whom four were African American, one was a recently naturalized citizen of Mexican heritage, with the remaining three representing the melting pot of European ancestry that had settled in the South since the early eighteen hundreds. Three of the eight were retired, five had college degrees, two had blue-collar jobs, and one of the women was a stay-at-home mom.

Picking juries was a tricky task, Allison had learned over the years. The information the attorneys were given about the jurors was minimal and received only shortly before jury selection, known in legal terms as voir dire, began. Attorneys had to trust their instincts based on answers they posed to prospective jurors. Allison felt pretty good about the eight people who would be deciding the Allied Plastics case, but she also knew that juries were unpredictable. All she could do was put on the best defense possible for her client.

Allison and Matt Aiken responded in the affirmative to Judge Lee's question, "Are counsels ready?" Aiken then called his client to the stand.

The first fifteen minutes of the plaintiff's testimony held no surprises. Matt Aiken walked his client through his work history with Allied Plastics, allowing the plaintiff ample leeway to tell the jury his side of the story. Matt Aiken's next question, however, caught Allison's attention as she heard the lie in the plaintiff's reply.

"Have you ever been accused of sexual harassment before the incident Allied Plastics claims you committed, Mr. Allen?" Matt Aiken slouched slightly against the lectern and smiled at his client.

"Absolutely not," the plaintiff replied earnestly. "This is the first time anyone has accused me of that sort of behavior."

Allison reached for the red rope file to her left. It was in there somewhere, she was sure of it. Listening with part of her brain and searching for the document she needed with the other, Allison smiled as she pulled Steve Allen's employment record from Maybell Dairies. Prior to starting with Allied Plastics, the plaintiff had worked as the HR director for a small dairy operation in the Midwest. The employment records had been provided to Allison and her client as part of a document request during discovery. *Matt should have paid closer attention.* Allison suppressed a smile as she placed the prior employment record on the top of the list of questions she intended to ask the plaintiff on cross-examination.

"Your witness," Judge Lee informed Allison several minutes later after Matt Aiken advised the judge that he was tendering his client for cross-examination.

Allison moved briskly to the lectern, opened her black trial notebook to the tab marked "Plaintiff's Cross," and per court protocol introduced herself to the plaintiff with a smile.

"Mr. Allen," she began, "I have of course been listening to your testimony as your attorney has questioned you this morning. Am I correct that you have testified that you have never—before the incident which caused your firing by my client—that you have never been accused of sexual harassment?" Allison gazed innocently at the man sitting in the witness booth next to Judge Lee.

"That's right," the plaintiff retorted. "Never."

"May I approach, Your Honor?" Allison asked for permission. Receiving an affirmative nod from Judge Lee, Allison retrieved the employment record from the trial notebook. "I've got only the one copy," Allison advised Matt Aiken as she turned to approach the witness box, "but you should have a copy in your files."

"Mr. Allen, I am handing you a document that you and your attorney provided me during discovery in this case. Isn't it true"—Allison handed the employment record to the plaintiff—"that you were accused of sexual harassment six years ago when you were the HR director at Maybell Dairies?"

Deer in the headlights was about the right expression that crossed the plaintiff's face, prefacing a whispered, "This was never proved."

"And that would be because you quit your job at Maybell Dairies after that employee brought the claim against you, isn't it?"

Getting no reply other than a hateful glare from the witness box, Allison pressed, "Isn't that correct, Mr. Allen? You left Maybell before an investigation could take place, didn't you?"

"I left," came a sullen reply. "Had my own reasons." Steve Allen crossed his arms at his chest in a defiant manner. A barely perceptible smile briefly touched Allison's face.

"Mr. Allen," Allison continued, "isn't it true that you told several female employees at Allied that you like your coffee like you like your women, that being 'hot and black'?"

The plaintiff's scowl deepened. "Yes," he replied.

Allison flipped several pages in her trial notebook, giving the appearance of searching for some item of interest. "And isn't it also true that you told a female security guard that 'once you go black, you can't go back'?"

"My wife is African American," the plaintiff retorted.

"And do you think that gives you permission to make racial comments to other women of color?" Allison barely got the question out of her mouth before Matt Aiken jumped to his feet with a loud "Objection, Your Honor."

"I'll withdraw the question," Allison responded quickly, aware that the jury would remember her inquiry even without the plaintiff's response.

By the time Allison had finished her cross-examination of the plaintiff, the clock over the courtroom's double doors showed four in the afternoon. Judge Lee hardly ever ran court past four thirty unless a trial was getting ready to conclude. This first day of trial had seen only one witness, the plaintiff, testify. Allison knew from the pretrial submissions that Matt Aiken intended to call several other witnesses, so Judge Lee's decision to adjourn for the day had come as no surprise. "Court will reconvene in the morning at nine," the judge had advised the parties.

Trial work was both invigorating and exhausting for Allison. When Allison walked into the courtroom the next morning, she was running on pure adrenaline, her few hours of sleep in her hotel room a faint memory. Given the amount of time her opponent had spent questioning his own client, Allison figured Matt Aiken would take the better part of the second day of trial putting on the rest of his witnesses. However, one could never be sure what would happen during a trial, so Allison had spent the early part of the preceding evening prepping two of her main defense witnesses in case the plaintiff rested his case before the end of the day. It had been midnight before she picked up her trial notebook to review the cross-examination questions she had previously prepared for the plaintiff's remaining witnesses.

"All rise," intoned Judge Lee's bailiff, and the second day of trial began.

Matt Aiken's strongest witness, at least in Allison's estimation, was the numbers man Matt had listed as an expert witness to testify about the plaintiff's alleged damages. In Steve Allen's case, damages consisted of the income he claimed to have lost after being fired and unable to find a job at the same pay he had made with Allied, plus monies the plaintiff claimed he had to spend seeking psychological counseling as a result of his wrongful firing. Allison didn't think much of Allen's claim for mental distress, but if the jury believed the plaintiff's claims, Allison's client was looking not only at actual damages but also punitive damages, which were recoverable in a whistle-blowing case like the one the plaintiff had brought. Allison did the best she could to chip away at the money man's calculations and the basis for his opinions, but it was difficult to successfully attack reality—the plaintiff had not been able to find comparable employment after his termination from Allied.

At three in the afternoon, Matt Aiken informed Judge Lee that he rested his case. Allison was glad she had prepared for this possibility. "Call your first witness," Judge Lee instructed Allison.

Allison had spent considerable time contemplating the order in which she would call her witnesses. Experience had taught her that putting your strongest witness on first was often a mistake in a jury trial. When the jury retired to deliberate, Allison wanted her best testimony to still be fresh in the jurors' minds.

"The defendant calls Kemper Bradley." Allison nodded to the president and CEO of Allied Plastics as he took the witness stand. In federal court, the scope of cross-examination was limited to the facts testified to by the witness on direct examination. Allison had no intention of opening the doors to irrelevant or extraneous information, so her examination was short and direct. Kemper Bradley testified about Allied's sexual harassment policy, told the jury why the plaintiff was terminated, and assured the jury that Allied had complied with all federal and state employment laws. When she tendered the CEO to Matt Aiken for cross-examination, there wasn't much for Matt to attack. The best Aiken had been able to do was make a disbelieving "Is that so?" retort to one of Kemper Bradley's answers.

Judge Lee had allowed the lawyers to complete the examination of Kemper Bradley that afternoon rather than hold the witness's testimony open overnight. During trial, time passes unnoticed for most litigators, and Allison was no exception. When court was adjourned, Allison was surprised to see that it was after six o'clock. Gathering her trial notebook, the various exhibits she intended to introduce through her remaining witnesses, and sending a quick text to her husband, Allison headed back to her hotel room for what she hoped was the last night of trial.

Allison pitched a softball witness to open the third day of trial. Mekesha Simmons was the Allied employee who had filed the sexual harassment charge against the plaintiff. Mekesha's quiet demeanor and soft voice immediately drew the jurors' attention. Allison doubted anyone on the jury would think that Mekesha Simmons had encouraged the plaintiff's attentions. When Matt Aiken took an overbearing approach on cross-examination, the young black woman began to weep. *Big mistake, Matt,* Allison thought. *What on earth were you thinking?*

The examination of Allison's next two witnesses was brief. Annabelle McFarlane and Justin Smith were called to corroborate Mekesha's story about the plaintiff's harassment. "Nothing from the plaintiff, Your Honor," Aiken had replied each time Allison tendered her morning's witnesses. Not cross-examining the opposing party's witnesses was a dangerous tactic. Allison wondered if Matt Aiken had a surprise rebuttal witness whom he thought would be more effective than cross-examining the eye witnesses to his client's behavior. Rebuttal witnesses didn't have to be disclosed to the other side before trial. Allison made a note to consider that possibility during the next break.

After Allison had released Justin Smith from the witness stand, advising Judge Lee she had "no further questions for the witness," Judge Lee called for the lunch recess.

"I'll be reconvening court at half past the hour," Judge Lee warned Allison and Matt. "Be ready with your next witness, Ms. Parker. I want to finish this trial before evening."

Allison had, in fact, saved her best witness for last. Alicia Cane was an African American woman who had retired as an army sergeant before her second career with Allied. Hired as an equal employment specialist, one of Alicia Cane's duties was to conduct remedial training for Allied employees who violated company policies or procedures. Exhibiting a tough, no-nonsense manner, Alicia turned a serious face toward the jury before answering Allison's question. "There's no way he didn't understand Allied's rules against sexual harassment," Allison's star witness had told the jury. "I made certain he knew if he ever did anything against policy again, no matter how slight, he was gone." Given the expressions on their faces, Allison knew the jurors had believed every word of Alicia Cane's testimony. Matt Aiken made an aggressive attempt at cross-examination, but he was no match for the twenty-year army veteran.

By three o'clock, Allison was laying out the facts of the case and pointing out the crucial pieces of testimony that the jury should consider. "The plaintiff is a serial harasser," Allison argued in her closing statement to the jury, reminding the eight men and women of the plaintiff's transgressions at Maybell Dairies. "He just doesn't get it." Allison urged the jury to deny the plaintiff any recovery and to bring back a defense verdict for her client. Five hours after Judge Lee dismissed the jury for deliberation, that's exactly what the jury foreman announced.

"Lord, I wish you could have seen Matt Aiken's face when his client admitted the previous harassment charge." Allison laughed from her reclining position on her office sofa the day after trial ended. "How he missed those records from Maybell Dairies is beyond me."

"You know how he missed them," David Jackson replied. "He had some paralegal pull everything together and then he never looked at the documents before they were sent to you."

"Or apparently before trial, for that matter." Allison stretched her arms over her head and gave a big yawn. "Late nights before trial are the least attractive part of getting prepared, but they sure are worth it when you come across a jewel like this. To be honest, I missed it the first time I went through those records, too," Allison admitted. "I think both sides were so focused on what had transpired at Allied and the whistle-blowing charge that neither one of us spent much time looking at the plaintiff's prior employment. I'm just grateful I took a closer look that last night and that I had that folder with me in the courtroom."

David Jackson pushed himself from the comfortable club chair in front of Allison's desk. "It's the tiny details that make the difference. Can't remember how many times you've told me so."

"You know, the odd thing about this case," Allison continued, "and what the plaintiff's testimony today really brought home to me is, I don't think the plaintiff saw anything wrong with the things he said to those women. How someone trained as a human resources director could think like that is incomprehensible to me."

David grinned, stopping at Allison's office door. "Trial work is never dull." Giving his partner a salute, David added, "Congratulations on a great win. But now, I'm the one with work to do. Catch you later," he called, heading toward his office.

"Donna," Allison called out, unwilling to leave the comfort of the soft corduroy sofa, "any fires I need to put out before I head to the house?"

Donna Pevey appeared at Allison's doorway. "No need to shout," she reprimanded her boss. "I ain't hard of hearing. I was on my way in here when David left." Handing her boss a small sheaf of pink slips, she added, "Just Frank. The rest can wait till tomorrow. Frank asked me to tell you he really needs to talk to you—sooner rather than later." Rolling her eyes, Donna added, "Everything's an emergency with that man."

"When you come as close to dying as Frank did, I imagine it changes your perspective on things," Allison remarked. "He's obsessed with Sean McIntosh's case right now. Not sure if it's because Sean is family or because the errand Sean admitted to sending Frank on nearly cost him his life."

Mollified, Donna gave Allison a sheepish grin. "Yeah, I know. God love him. Well, give him a call will you, even if you just leave a message? That way, I'll have done my duty getting Frank's message to you."

"I'll call him from the car." Silently, Allison hoped Frank wouldn't answer. A stack of zees had her name on them.

CHAPTER
TWENTY-FOUR

Nine Months Ago

Plato McCall was an angry man. His family had conspired against him, his business partners had conspired against him, Hell, even life had conspired against him. Plato swore profusely in English and then in Gaelic. His family he could do without. Who needed a bunch of whiny pussies? He'd taken the family business and quadrupled its value, only to be fired by the board of directors—all siblings or cousins—because his "business plan" had exposed the company to criminal liability. Ingrates, every one of them. Oh, they'd paid him off under the table, and very handsomely indeed, to get rid of him without a fuss and as evidence to assure the authorities that Plato had acted outside the scope of his authority and without the knowledge or approval of anyone else in the company. *More likely to save their shitty little asses*, Plato thought, remembering the events of twenty years earlier. Whatever the board's intentions, Plato was served up as the sacrificial lamb. Even after paying off the Boston judge and district attorney, Plato had been forced to accept a plea deal that included eighteen months in a white-collar federal prison.

Never a man to miss an opportunity, even one he would have preferred to have come across in a different manner, Plato spent his prison time fruitfully. Utilizing the prison library's computers, installed to provide the inmates a sense of "normalcy" after an ACLU lawsuit complained about prisoner's rights, Plato McCall emerged a free man with a plan. A plan to punish those who had put him behind bars, who had stripped him of his rightful place in society, who had condemned him to wear forever the name of felon.

Killing his cousin Jamison McCall had been easier than Plato expected. Making it appear an accident had been a bit worrisome, but by the time the body had washed ashore, all the coroner could definitively state was that Jamison McCall had drowned. Not one had been around the night Plato had used the hidden key to access Jamison's beach house on the cape, knocked his cousin unconscious, and tossed him into the ocean. If Plato's attack had left any signs, the sea and its inhabitants had long extinguished the marks by the time the remains were discovered by the unfortunate woman walking her dog.

Time was irrelevant to Plato in the execution of his plan. Only success mattered. Plato waited patiently. Taking Ian Standish would be much more difficult. A second cousin on Plato's mother's side and CEO of McCall Enterprises after Plato's ignominious ouster, Ian Standish was a man of few pleasures. Neither alcohol nor tobacco had ever touched Ian Standish's chaste lips, and given Ian's unmarried status, Plato figured his cousin's dick was as pristine as his lips. Two years after Jamison's murder, Plato found Ian's weakness.

Actually, it wasn't much of a weakness if you had the money to indulge yourself. Ian Standish's weakness was gliders—as in unmotorized, hanging from a flimsy concoction of wood and fabric, hang gliding. Plato had stumbled across his cousin's new hobby purely by accident. He knew better than to be seen in and around Boston anymore. Plato's access to money was tied to his agreement to stay away from Boston and from any member of the family. The funds regularly deposited in the Cayman account were Plato's sole means of accomplishing his objective and added a delicious irony to his schemes against the family—his victims were financing their own deaths. Plato would not jeopardize his income stream, no matter how tempting it was to walk the streets of the town he so sorely missed.

In the end, paying the thug to break into the private airstrip and sabotage Ian's glider wasn't nearly as satisfying as doing it himself, but Plato wasn't sure the glider would actually crash, or if it did, whether Ian would die. If unsuccessful, Plato needed an alibi in case anyone looked his way.

The breaking news on WCVB confirmed the worst for Ian and the best for Plato. *Local businessman and philanthropist dies in glider accident.* Two down and one to go. Plato had smiled watching the report. A few days later, Plato rewarded the thug with an extra five grand, thanked him for a job well done, then capped him with a GLOCK .19 when the hired man turned away to count his unexpected bonus. Plato didn't need complications. No one would miss the lowlife, and Plato doubted the police would bother with much of an investigation, assuming they found the body any time soon.

Plato had decided to savor his last kill. Daphne McCall MacGregor. Plato's baby sister and the bitch who had sold him out to the rest of the family. Killing her quickly was out of the question. Torturing her first, giving her the hope of salvation, pushing his sister to the brink of insanity—Plato's mouth had watered thinking of the exquisite pleasure he would obtain with this last piece of revenge.

He had planned carefully. Eight years had passed since Plato had walked the streets of the town from which he had been banned. It wasn't enough to have killed Jamison and Ian. It wouldn't be enough to kill Daphne. True revenge, Plato believed, would only be achieved when he could take his rightful place among his peers. Oh, he'd still take care of Daphne. Those who had betrayed him would suffer justice as defined by Plato McCall. Daphne would not be an exception. But after he had conducted the final execution, Plato intended to resume the life that had been so unfairly taken from him.

The contacts Plato had made in prison proved quite helpful in obtaining a second identity, using a false name to buy a small cottage in remote upstate New York and to order or purchase the various items he would need to accomplish his goal of inflicting the utmost pain possible on the sister he despised before killing her. Secure in the knowledge that neither the cottage nor any of his purchases could be traced back to him, Plato had made every criminal's mistake. He became careless.

Plato made his move against his sister on a balmy Sunday morning in March. The hint of an early spring had encouraged many Bostonians to sample the sunshine, including a man who was taking an early exercise run. Sean McIntosh had just rounded the corner onto Tremont Street when he heard a woman scream. Running toward the sounds of distress, Sean acted instinctively to tackle the large man who was attempting to push a struggling woman into a nearby car. Later, Sean would tell the police that luck must have been with him that day. The momentum of Sean's tackle had carried both men into a nearby US Postal Service mailbox, knocking Plato McCall unconscious. By the time Daphne McGregor's brother regained consciousness, he was cuffed and in the back of a police cruiser.

This time, Plato's prison sentence was longer. Twelve to fifteen years was the incarceration period the judge had handed down, with credit for time served while Plato had awaited trial. This time, his quarters weren't as comfortable either. The state prison in Cedar Junction, Massachusetts—formerly known as MCI-Walpole—was a maximum-security prison housing approximately eight hundred male inmates at any given time. One of two maximum security facilities in the commonwealth, over the years the facility had hosted its share of (in)famous criminals. Albert DeSalvo, the Boston Strangler, was incarcerated there until he was murdered in prison by persons unknown, as was John Salvi, an abortion opponent who killed two people and wounded five others in shootings at two Planned Parenthood clinics in 1994.

Cedar Junction changed Plato McCall. Incarceration with hardened criminals eroded what spark of redemption might have lingered in Plato's soul. His sister's death from cancer five years into Plato's sentence had enraged him. Getting out of prison and finishing his mission had been Plato's consuming passion, removing him mentally from the daily grind of prison life. For months, he had become despondent, refusing food, withdrawing further into himself. Then, he remembered the man. The do-gooder who had interfered. It was his fault that Plato had been stopped, had been caught, had been convicted. A new plan began to emerge, a plan that had given Plato McCall a reason to live in prison, a reason to plan for the future.

Ten years into his sentence, Plato received a reprieve. Overcrowding had forced the Massachusetts prison system to reevaluate its inmates' status. Those near the end of their sentences who had shown remorse or rehabilitation were recommended for early release. During his decade at Cedar Junction, Plato had kept to himself, toed the line, and become as invisible as possible. When the parole board named the list of prisoners to be released, Plato's name was included.

Upon his release, Plato began his research on Sean McIntosh. To Plato's surprise, Sean McIntosh did not live in Boston. It had been simple bad luck that had put a visiting Sean McIntosh on Tremont Street that day for his daily run. It had taken a while to figure out his plan. All Plato knew for sure was that killing McIntosh would require careful planning. A third felony strike would put Plato McCall away for life. Whatever happened, Plato McCall knew going back to prison was not an option for him. Sean McIntosh's punishment would have to be different, creative, and final.

Plato's Cayman accounts had remained untouched during his years behind bars. The sharp intelligence that had allowed Plato McCall to enlarge the coffers of McCall Enterprises when he had run the company had served him well as he directed investments from his prison cell via his Cayman broker. By the time he became a free man once again, Plato McCall was worth many millions.

The cottage Plato had purchased in upstate New York as an intended hidey-hole for torturing and killing his sister, Daphne, now morphed into a high-tech research center. Money had a way of opening doors that would otherwise be closed, and it had not taken long for Plato to amass a fairly detailed dossier on his target. When he discovered Sean's relationship with Maria Sanchez, Plato knew he'd found McIntosh's Achilles' heel.

The small ranch near Gainesville had crossed Plato's radar a couple of months earlier—close enough for him to keep an eye on his targets, far enough to not be seen or recognized, and cheap enough for him to buy outright. Running into his childhood friend Joanie Bradley at the Gainesville Costco had been a shock—Plato had intended to stay as incognito as possible—but Joanie had introduced him to her husband, Blake, engaged in the kind of small talk that Plato remembered from his Boston days, and had bought Plato's cover story about why he was now living in the area. Although he had promised to stay in touch, Plato had no intention of further contact with Joanie or her husband. The Tellers were busy breeding race horses. Soon, Plato figured, they would forget all about him.

CHAPTER TWENTY-FIVE

Present Day

Evelyn Goodpasture was despondent and angry. How these two emotions could live side by side within her being was a mystery to her. All she knew was that one moment she was so sad she could barely function and the next, she was so furious that murder seemed the only antidote to her agony.

The social opprobrium that had resulted from her divorce trial didn't bother Evelyn in the least. Those people Miles hung around with had never held her interest. Shallow and uneducated was her assessment of the monied crowd in Fort Charles. The fact that most of those residents were college graduates and that some even held advanced degrees was of no consequence to Evelyn. Education, true education, required a native intelligence that Evelyn found lacking in those whose extracurricular activities revolved around alcohol, parties, and achieving social status.

Having to give up her house hadn't bothered her either. The house Miles had insisted they buy when his business took off was garish in Evelyn's estimation. Too big, too fancy, too much of everything Evelyn had come to disdain. Moving from that monstrosity had been more relief than regret. The small duplex near the college would serve her sufficiently. Miles had been generous in allowing Evelyn to take what furniture she had wanted primarily, she surmised, because it gave Miles an excuse to buy new and more expensive furniture rather than any desire on his part to be kind.

What bothered Evelyn Goodpasture and what caused her emotions to rage wildly from one extreme to the other had nothing to do with how the divorce and its publicity affected *her*. No, what really bothered Evelyn was the damage that the exposé of her sex life had done to Pierre Chastain and Mavis Johnson and to a lesser extent, to the other men who had been her sexual partners.

Pierre had been fired from his job as a teacher at the local private academy; the board of trustees invoked a morals clause in Pierre's employment contract. Being fired on a morals charge was the end of Pierre Chastain's teaching career. Finding a job in the education business would be near impossible. Pierre had not contacted Evelyn since the divorce trial, and given his recent firing, Evelyn knew she would never see or hear from him again. If Pierre had any chance of starting over, it would have to be far from Fort Charles and the state of Alabama.

As much as Evelyn enjoyed sex with Pierre, she had yearned for more. If sex with one man was good, wouldn't sex with more than one be even better? After discovering the existence of several swingers sites on the Internet, Evelyn had been able to make contact with two men who advertised themselves as "Masters" in the world of sex fantasy. Dwight England and Pete Hubbard satisfied Evelyn in an erotic threesome that exceeded her expectations. Never had she felt so alive, so accepted, so wanted. Being taken from behind by Dwight while Pete sucked her breasts had only been the beginning. The four times they had met over as many months had awakened a sexual fire in Evelyn. No sexual act was off limits, no act too depraved. The publicity from the trial wouldn't hurt Dwight and Pete—as far as they were concerned, it was all free publicity—but Evelyn would not be able to afford their company any longer on pittance of alimony that Judge Kaufman had ordered Miles to pay.

But the damage inflicted on Mavis Johnson was the worst. A Sunday school teacher in nearby Eufala, Alabama, Mavis had not waited to be fired, shunned, or expelled from her church. Evelyn's call after Frank Martin's surveillance films were shown in court had been all the motivation Mavis needed. The note found by the Barbour County sheriff said it all: *You promised no one would know.* Evelyn didn't need to ask. She knew the note was intended for her.

What had happened to her wasn't fair. Miles was the one who had screwed around for years. She was sure of it. Evelyn paced the living room of the small apartment remembering her conversations with her divorce attorney.

"You don't have any proof, Evelyn," her attorney had explained. "It doesn't do your case any good to allege Miles was unfaithful if we can't produce evidence to support our accusations."

"Everyone in Fort Charles knows he cheated on me," Evelyn had insisted. "Just ask around."

Mark Lockridge had made a halfhearted attempt to find such a witness, but as he'd expected, Fort Charles society had already closed ranks against Evelyn. The couple's friends had made a choice, and it wasn't Evelyn. "I've talked to everyone I can think of who might have information about Miles's extra-curricular activities," Lockridge reported. "No go. If anyone knows anything, they are not sharing it with me. A counterclaim for infidelity is out of the question, at least if I am representing you. I can't file a complaint with an allegation I know I can't prove at trial. It's unethical."

Picking up a small vase on a nearby table, Evelyn heaved the delicate container as hard as she could. The sound of shattering glass filled the silence of the small abode. Evelyn stared at the mess she had made. Violence wouldn't serve her, not right now. Evelyn moved to the small dining table, pulled out a chair and sat. Evelyn's journal lay open where she had left it the night before. Pierre was still young. He would find work somewhere, even if he had to change careers. He would survive because he was a man, and in the end, society would pat Pierre Chastain on the head and say, "Boys will be boys." Evelyn understood Mavis's decision to take her own life. Society would never have been accepting of Mavis's conduct, not in small-town Alabama, no matter how many states passed same-sex marriage laws. Taking up her pen, Evelyn began to write. Someone would pay.

CHAPTER TWENTY-SIX

Expressing his satisfaction with the Big Boy special, Frank Martin let out a loud belch. That young doctor likely meant well, but Frank was feeling a whole lot better now that he had returned to his normal eating habits. He and Dr. Lopez had argued about Frank's diet at his last appointment in Birmingham.

"I can't eat like a damn bird," Frank had complained. "It's unnatural."

"Mr. Martin, if you don't change your dietary habits and lose at least thirty pounds, you're going to die a lot sooner than you'd like." Dr. Lopez's tone had reminded Frank of old Ms. Rankin, his third-grade teacher.

"I'll try," was all Frank could bring himself to offer the young doctor.

Frank *had* tried, for a week or two, with the result that he lost five pounds and was starving all the time. Greek yogurt and fruit for breakfast, lean meat and a veggie for lunch, same again for dinner—unappetizing and bland. *What was the use of eating anything if you couldn't enjoy it?* Frank asked himself. Then, this morning, Frank had reached his limit. The pittance of breakfast food had done nothing to assuage his hunger. Grabbing his keys, Frank drove the short distance from his house to the diner and ordered his favorite breakfast.

Frank was savoring his third cup of coffee when a bell jangled as Sheriff Toby Trowbridge pushed open the diner's front door. "Hey, Toby," Frank hailed the sheriff. "Want to join me?"

Toby slid into Frank's booth. "Nina, just the regular," the sheriff called to the waitress who had headed in his direction. Turning his attention to Frank, Toby asked, "What's up?"

"Good to see you, too." Frank grinned in reply. "I don't get a 'How are you?' or such?"

"I'm not blind, Martin." Toby laughed. "By the look of all this mess on the table, I'd say you're doing just fine."

"Ha, that I am," Frank agreed, "but running into you here saves me tracking you down later today.

Have you made any progress on figuring out who shot me?"

"Thanks, Nina." The sheriff nodded at the waitress who placed a bowl of oatmeal and wheat toast in front of Toby.

"How can you eat that shit?" Frank asked.

"Under two hundred calories, four grams of protein. Wouldn't want to guess how many calories were in that meal you just consumed. Besides," Toby added, "I like oatmeal." Pointing at the empty plates in front of Frank, Toby asked, "I thought you were supposed to be losing weight?"

"I've lost ten pounds." Frank fudged on the number. "Time to reward myself." Frank motioned to Nina for a refill on his coffee. "I didn't ask you to sit with me to discuss my weight." Frank scowled. "Where are you on catching whoever tried to kill me?"

"No closer than I was a month ago. Whoever it was, man or woman, no prints were left at the scene, at least none we could pull. Sean McIntosh thinks they were after him, not you, but I've hit a dead end there as well," the sheriff admitted. "Allison told me you'd gone back to McIntosh Farms for a few days. You have any better luck?"

"Nothing concrete yet, but there's something Sean is hiding." Frank drained the last of his refilled coffee. "Not sure if it has anything to do with the case, but my nose tells me it probably does."

"What do you think McIntosh is hiding?" Toby was curious. McIntosh had seemed pretty forthright the two times he had spoken with the man.

"I stayed down at Sean's ranch for three days. Talked to all his ranch hands, spent my evenings talking to Sean about everything I could think of that might shed light on what happened to me as well as the horse Sean says was stolen from him. I think he's right about the two being connected—whoever shot me expected Sean—but that doesn't tell me why someone would steal Blue Scarlet." Frank picked up the ticket Nina had left for him. "Best cheap eats in town," he remarked, reaching for his wallet.

"So, I'll ask again," the sheriff interrupted, "what do you think McIntosh is hiding?"

"One of his ranch hands, Jorge Velasquez, mentioned a bodega, said the woman who runs it used to live at the ranch," Frank replied. "It's not much of a lead, but Sean never mentioned her to me. We talked about lots of things, not just the stolen horse. The fact that Sean never mentioned this woman makes me suspicious."

"Did you talk to her while you were in Bell?"

"No. Thought the direct approach wasn't maybe the best." Frank considered whether he should share his plan. "Thought I'd talk to Allison. Get her ideas about how to approach the woman."

"You'd better be careful what you ask Allison to get involved with," Toby cautioned. "The last two times y'all worked a case together..." The look he gave Frank provided an unspoken warning. "I don't think Jim Kaufman will be so forgiving a third time."

"All I'm gonna do is get her opinion on some stuff," Frank prevaricated. "Besides, she's already been to Sean's place once before and nothing happened."

"Nothing happened?" Toby exclaimed. "I heard y'all interrupted a fight, and Allison drew her gun to break it up. I don't think that qualifies as 'nothing happened.'"

"You know what I mean," Frank argued. "Nothing happened to Allison. And tossing around my suspicions about the case ain't gonna make anything happen either." At least that was Frank's hope.

"Well, let me know what you decide to do, Frank," the sheriff ordered. "I don't want either one of you going off half-cocked just to test out one of your theories."

"Yeah, yeah," Frank murmured, leaving the booth.

"I mean it, Frank." Toby raised his voice to follow Frank's retreating back. "I don't want to hear about it after the fact."

A dismissive wave of Frank's hand as he exited the diner was the only response. *At least he heard me,* the sheriff thought, *although Lord knows if he'll heed my warning.*

CHAPTER
TWENTY-SEVEN

"I'm going to run down to Bell with Frank on Monday to have a chat with a woman Frank thinks may have some information about Sean McIntosh." Allison raised her voice over the sound of the hairdryer she was holding. "Can you be home by five to let Sharon go?"

Jim Kaufman stepped out of the shower, took the noise maker from his wife's hand, and clicked the Off button. "I can hear you better without that inferno interference. What did you say?"

The large mirror over the double vanity reflected her husband's unclothed body. Standing a hair under six feet, Jim Kaufman's athletic build and flat abs belied the double nickels that would mark his next birthday. A familiar fluttering sensation flickered in Allison's belly, accompanied by a hot wetness between her legs. Allison's question fled her mind. Turning, she let her bathrobe fall to the floor.

Jim's erection was instantaneous as Allison knelt before her husband and pulled his hardness into her mouth. Grabbing his taut buttocks, Allison strained to take all of her husband's penis. "Oh God," Jim moaned, pushing his hands through his wife's long hair as his penis began to pulsate toward a building release. "Not yet," he commanded, pulling himself away from Allison. "Together."

The plush pile of their bedroom carpet embraced the couple as their breathing became rapid and ragged. Allison locked her legs around her husband's body, accepting his weight and his manhood, drenching herself and her husband in the juices that flowed as she opened herself in ecstasy to the man she loved with all her heart. They climaxed together, a blending of the physical and spiritual, made perfect by their union.

Afterward, Allison rested her head on her husband's chest. "It never gets old." She smiled.

"No, it doesn't," Jim agreed, giving his wife a soft kiss. "But I swear, woman, one of these days, this is likely to kill me," he concluded with a laugh.

"Can't think of a finer way to go out," Allison re-marked, "but you better not be planning on going anywhere any time soon."

"Don't worry, babe. I plan to be around for a long, long time," her husband replied. Jim stood, reached a hand to help Allison from the floor. "What did you ask me before we were otherwise engaged?"

"Let me get cleaned up while you dress. I'll ex-plain over breakfast." Donning a cap to protect her hair, Allison hopped into the shower.

Fifteen minutes later, as her children happily at-tacked a stack of pancakes Jim had prepared, Allison joined her family around the large breakfast table. "Good thing it's summer break," Allison observed. "If Charlotte and Mack were headed to school after consuming all this sugar, I'm sure I'd hear about it from one or both of their teachers."

"Mama, you know I don't get in trouble at school," Mack reminded Allison. "I know better."

"That you do, my good boy," Allison agreed. "Now, if you and Charlotte are finished, y'all need to go out to the barn and feed the horses. Sharon will be here soon, and chores need to be done if you want to go to the park today." A brief touch of mayhem rocked the kitchen as Charlotte and Mack wolfed down the remains of their breakfast, bolted from the table, and raced out of the house. "Careful," Allison called after her progeny, silently acknowledging the futility of her request and grateful that serious injury had so far escaped her children notwithstanding their propensity to test the limits of safe activities.

Seeing his wife's face, Jim offered his standard bit of wisdom. "They'll be fine, Allison. Don't worry so much."

"I know," Allison replied, savoring the short stack Jim placed in front of her. "It's just the mother in me. By the way, these pancakes are just divine. Wish I could indulge like this every day."

"Don't see why you can't." Jim grinned. "You just have to start off with the same appetizer to justify the calories."

"Fine by me." Allison smirked. "But I'm not sure you'd be able to keep up."

"Very funny," Jim replied, "but unfortunately probably true, too."

"Use it or lose it," Allison reminded her husband. "I'm not worried about you or your stamina." A sip of lukewarm coffee caused Allison's lips to pucker. "Yuck," she remarked, shaking her head. "Anyway, let me tell you about my plans for Monday."

Jim warmed Allison's coffee, poured a cup for himself, and waited. The fact that Allison was sharing her plans with him meant she wasn't headed into any sort of trouble. At least he hoped not.

Allison began by summarizing what she and Frank had discovered so far. "Frank talked to Toby the other day. Toby's no further ahead on finding Frank's attacker than he was at the beginning of the investigation. Frank thinks his attacker is tied to Sean McIntosh in some fashion, but Toby has his doubts." Allison placed the morning's dirty dishes in the dishwasher as she continued. "Frank spent several days at Sean's ranch last week. He's convinced there's something Sean is hiding, and he's pretty certain it has something to do with a woman who is running a bodega outside Bell."

"A woman running a bodega?" Jim interrupted. "Where did Frank get this idea?"

"I asked Frank the same question." Allison nodded. "It sounded rather far out to me. But Frank said one of Sean's ranch hands told him Sean and this woman were tight. You know Frank. That was enough to make him curious."

"So has he talked to this mystery woman?" Jim pressed.

"That's just it," Allison explained. "Frank said Sean never mentioned the woman. Said Sean was wide open about everything else, but never said a thing about a relationship with anyone. According to the ranch hand, the woman actually lived at the ranch for a while."

"Maybe Sean didn't think his personal life was any of Frank's business," Jim remarked. "I can certainly understand why McIntosh wouldn't have mentioned someone he was sleeping with, especially if the relationship had terminated."

"According to the ranch hand, Sean is still in contact with this woman, even set her up in business," Allison replied. "I tend to agree with Frank on this one. Whoever this woman is, she deserves some investigation."

"And that's where you come in, I assume?" Jim asked.

"Yes. Frank thinks she'll talk more willingly to another woman. He's asked me to ride down Monday and see what I can find out." The Viking dishwasher made a soft whirring sound as Allison started the cleaning cycle. "Not sure we'll discover much of anything, but Frank is determined to find out who shot him, and he has convinced himself that it's connected to his cousin. I figure it will be late Monday when we get back. So can you be here by five to let Sharon leave?"

"Won't be a problem," Jim assured his wife. "Just be careful. Things don't always turn out the way you expect when you and Frank are together."

CHAPTER
TWENTY-EIGHT

The power of money was just extraordinary. It opened doors, hired people, allowed secrets to be kept, and best of all, would allow Plato McCall to exact his last bit of revenge against those who had wronged him. Plato knew better than to trust that spic cunt Sean McIntosh had taken up with. Women like that, Plato was certain, would turn on their own offspring if it would save their scrawny asses. Plato figured the Sanchez woman was no exception. Sure, she'd seemed frightened and willing to do his bidding after he'd threatened her. And she had to a degree, getting him access to the ranch that night so he could steal the horse, but he'd sensed a hesitation when he'd made his next demand. Paying to have a wiretap placed on the bodega's phone had been a stroke of genius. He now knew Sean and Maria were going to Cullman to pick up the kid this weekend. Taking and killing the horse hadn't been enough revenge for Plato. His needs, along with his plans, had changed.

There wasn't time to find a good hidey-hole in Bell. Plato didn't like keeping his hostages at the ranch, but he couldn't see any other feasible option on such short notice. If he didn't act now, any opportunity for real revenge might well be lost to him going forward. Carefully, Plato prepared his shopping list: rope, syringes, box cutters with extra blades, heavy cloth for blindfolds and other bindings, knives, chloroform, lighter, gasoline. He spread out his purchases—one store in Ocala, another in Gainesville, one in Tampa. No need to make some clerk suspicious.

He'd gotten away with two murders, but he figured his name would top the list of suspects after the bodies were found at the ranch. That fat PI Sean had hired had left several phone messages on Plato's answering machine. Stupidly, but before he realized the extent of possible exposure, Plato had returned a call to a woman attorney. Thank God she hadn't been in her office. After he put two and two together, Plato had refused to answer or return any further calls from the PI or the lawyer.

When he had been released from prison the last time, Plato had spent a small fortune obtaining a new identity. He'd never used it; he just had all the paperwork, passport, driver's license, and other necessary documentation resting in his safety deposit box—insurance against a time he would need a quick getaway. Soon, the time would come to leave Plato McCall behind and become a new person, a person whom Plato McCall had graciously added to all of the Cayman bank accounts and who would have no difficulty at all in enjoying a new life outside the good old United States. Plato had debated whether to use his new identity when he rented the van he would use to finish this last job. If he used his real name, the authorities might have a clue that would prevent his ultimate escape. On the other hand, if he used his new identity, and somehow a connection was made to him, the future life he intended to enjoy would be jeopardized. Better to rent the van in his own name, Plato decided.

Saturday morning dawned cool and cloudless, a rarity for May in Florida. The drive from Bell, Florida, to Cullman, Alabama, and back would take Sean and Maria around seven and a half hours. From what he had gathered listening to the wiretapped conversation earlier in the week, Sean would pick up Maria at 6:00 a.m., get to Cullman by early afternoon, pick up the kid, and head straight back to Bell, arriving at the ranch late that night. Sean would be tired from driving; Maria would be distracted by her kid. Plato McCall would be waiting for them.

CHAPTER TWENTY-NINE

Toby Trowbridge skimmed the report FBI agent Jake Cleveland had e-mailed. Concerned about Frank's plan to have Allison act as a sleuth on the Sean McIntosh case, Toby had dropped by Allison's office the day before.

"I told Jim there's nothing to worry about." Allison was exasperated. "I'm telling you the same thing. All I'm going to do is have a nice, innocuous chat with the woman Frank thinks may have some information he can use."

"I know that's what you plan to do, but nothing is ever that simple when you and Frank are involved," the sheriff replied. "This investigation started with

Frank's attempted murder. We don't have the slightest clue about who tried to kill Frank. For all you know, it was this woman you and Frank are interviewing on Monday."

"This woman has a name—Maria Sanchez. According to Frank, Sean McIntosh probably had some sort of relationship with her, enough of one to set her up in business running that bodega. None of the employees Frank interviewed when he was at the ranch had anything negative to say about Maria," Allison explained.

"According to Frank, there was only one ranch hand who even mentioned this woman," Toby replied. "I think that, in and of itself, is suspicious, particularly if the woman actually lived at the ranch for a while like the ranch hand said."

Allison shook her head in disagreement. "Can't see it. Maria Sanchez may or may not be able to share some helpful information with us. We'll just have to see, but I don't picture her as a killer."

"Who else, then? There's just not a single potential suspect on the radar," Toby asked.

Allison reached into her desk drawer, removing a slim file. "The closest I've come to a suspect is a guy named Plato McCall." Allison opened the folder and flipped through several pages. "He's really not a suspect," she added, "just a person I would like to talk to. He won't return my calls or Frank's. I got his name from Jeri Kennedy. She said if anyone in the horse business would have background on Sean McIntosh, it would be this McCall guy."

A distant memory niggled in the back of Toby's brain. "That name sounds familiar. Have you run a check on him?"

"No. The only reason his name came up at all was as a resource." Allison handed the file to Toby. "Here's everything I have on him. You're welcome to take the file with you. Just get it back to me at some point. I think he's probably a dead end."

As soon as Toby returned to his office, he had called Jake Cleveland and asked for a favor. "I ran Plato McCall's name through the system. Saw he's got a record. First time, white-collar crime. Second time, aggravated assault and attempted murder. His name has come up peripherally in an investigation. I was hoping you could get more info on the guy for me."

"Let me guess"—Jake laughed—"Allison and Frank are in the middle of this, right?"

"I don't know if you heard about what happened to Frank. Someone tried to kill him while he was working on a case out of Florida. McCall's name has been mentioned as someone who might have intel on Frank's client, a guy named Sean McIntosh." Toby gave Jake a rundown on the events that had transpired after the night Frank was shot and Allison's current involvement. "I know you don't believe in co-incidences any more than I do."

"No, I sure don't," Jake interjected, "particularly when the so-called coincidence involves an ex-con. Let me see what I can find out for you."

What Jake Cleveland had found out about Plato McCall had been plenty. If the report from the FBI agent was accurate—and Toby had no reason to think otherwise—Plato McCall was a dangerous man. Reaching for his phone, Toby dialed.

"Good afternoon, Martin Investigations." Sheila McMurray's Alabama drawl lengthened the greeting to multiple syllables.

"Sheila, it's Sheriff Trowbridge," Toby identified himself. "Is Frank around?"

"I'm sorry, Sheriff, but Mr. Martin's gone for the weekend. He won't be back until Tuesday. He and Ms. Parker are going to be out of town on a case Monday."

"I'll try his cell," the sheriff advised the recep-tionist, "but please leave Frank a message to call me if he comes back to the office today. It's important."

"Yes, sir, Sheriff," Sheila replied. "I sure will."

Toby's call to Frank's cell had no better results. "Leave a message," Frank's rough voice ordered. "I'll call you back." Obeying Frank's recorded directive, Toby left as much a detailed message as possible, tell-ing Frank to call as soon as he could.

Toby knew he ought to call Allison. Based on his earlier conversation with her, Toby knew Allison had no idea who Plato McCall really was. The problem was, Toby knew Allison well, and there was no way she would let Plato McCall's past history deter her from helping Frank on the McIntosh case or in solving the mystery of who tried to kill Frank. Toby's best chance of getting Allison off the case was to appeal directly to Frank Martin. Frank wouldn't take any chances with Allison's safety. If there was even a possibility that Plato McCall was involved in the McIntosh case, Frank would leave Allison in Fort Charles.

The last person Toby considered calling was Allison's husband, Judge Kaufman. There wasn't a good outcome either way. If he called the judge and told him about Plato McCall and his suspicions about the man, Jim Kaufman would be sure to insist his wife cancel the trip to Bell. Allison would be out of any potential danger, but she would see Toby's tattling as just that and none of his business. The last time Toby had tried to use Jim Kaufman to run interference on a matter Allison was involved in, she had let him have it with both barrels.

"I'm not a child, dammit!" Allison's voice had boomed over Toby's office telephone line. "How dare you call my husband as if he could dictate what I do! I make my own decisions, and you better damn well remember that, Tobias Trowbridge." Toby cringed as he relived the memory of that unpleasant experience. "If you have something to say or some concern, say it to my face." It had been weeks before Allison had spoken to him. Toby wasn't afraid of Allison, at least not as he'd admit it, but he valued her friendship and he knew he had diminished her opinion of him by treating her as less than an equal.

On the other hand, if things in the McIntosh investigation went south and Allison got hurt, Toby didn't like to think about what Jim Kaufman would do if he discovered Toby had known of the potential danger and not told him. Judge Kaufman might be even tempered in the court room, but when it came to protecting his family, an entirely different person took over. Just last year, only the quick thinking of the judge's bailiff had stopped the judge from killing a man who had been attempting to rape Allison, and eighteen months before that, the judge had barely escaped with his own life trying to protect Allison in an FBI sting gone awry. No, Toby didn't like to contemplate that possibility either.

In the end, Toby decided Plato McCall was not a likely imminent threat. In fact, it seemed from what Allison had shared with him the day before, McCall was avoiding contact with Allison and Frank, more likely a sign he didn't want to get involved with law enforcement rather than anything suspicious. All

Allison and Frank were doing Monday was talking to a woman who may or may not have had a romantic relationship with Sean McIntosh. Plato McCall might deserve another look, but it could wait until Tuesday.

Toby decided to make one more call before he left the office. As before, Frank Martin's recorded order instructed Toby to leave a message. "Frank, it's Toby. I ran a man named Plato McCall, got a report on him from Jake Cleveland, too. If he's involved in the McIntosh matter, you need to be very careful. He's a nasty piece of work. Right now, I don't see a connection to your case, but Allison was curious about him. His last address was outside Gainesville. Just be careful."

CHAPTER THIRTY

E velyn Goodpasture was the epitome of a Southern woman in at least one aspect. She owned several firearms and knew how to use each one of them. A staunch supporter of the Second Amendment, Evelyn thought Charlton Heston had it right when he told an NRA convention that his gun would have to be pulled from his "cold, dead hands."

Evelyn also knew it was people, not guns, who killed. All that self-righteous blathering from the Left. How many of them, she wondered, would sing a different song if being armed could have saved them or their loved ones from serious harm or death? Even the current president, who preached gun control at every opportunity, had armed Secret Service agents around him all the time. *Hypocrite,* Evelyn thought as she drew the cleaning rod through the barrel of her handgun. *Fucking, weeny ass hypocrite.*

Evelyn sighted the gun away from her, taking care to check the chamber one more time, even though she had counted the bullets when she emptied the gun to clean it. *Clean as a whistle,* Evelyn thought, admiring her work. Placing the revolver on the kitchen table, Evelyn picked up the long rifle, the one she had been given by her grandfather on her sixteenth birthday. Evelyn had loved her grandpa Smith. A man of limited school learning, Beauregard Smith had educated himself via the small public library in Gadsden, Alabama, in the foothills of the Appalachians where he had been raised. Along with gifting a lifelong love of books to his only grandchild, Evelyn's grandfather had introduced her to the ascetic discipline of marksmanship. Shooting had been the perfect sport for Evelyn, one she could practice in solitude, answering only to the marks on the shooting-range target, or rewarded by the deer she had taken down during hunting season.

Disassembling the long rifle was tedious but necessary work. Evelyn had not decided which weapon she would use to take out the man who had caused her such pain. Her plan was not yet complete. Her choice of weapon would be dependent on where she planned to make her attack. Whether she would escape after she completed her task was a scenario that Evelyn did not want to consider. All that needed to concern her now, she told herself, was to clean all of her guns, make sure she had sufficient ammunition for each of them, and then begin to study the routine of her target. The time and place would reveal themselves to her. All Evelyn had to do was wait. When she accomplished her mission, no one would think that the gun had killed anyone. Everyone would know who had pulled the trigger and why.

It was early evening by the time Evelyn had cleaned the last of her four guns. Taking care not to mar the shining barrels with her fingerprints, Evelyn wrapped each weapon in soft cloth. A baby could not have had a gentler swaddling. An aching back caught Evelyn's attention, causing her to stand and stretch as best she could. She should have taken a break earlier in the day. Five hours hunched over her weaponry, cleaning the minutest part, putting the guns back together—all of this had conspired to aggravate the back injury that had plagued Evelyn for the past several years. Her body's weakness infuriated Evelyn. She had work to do and no time to waste. Gulping down a tumbler of tap water, Evelyn swallowed three Aleve pills and opened her laptop.

Initially, Evelyn had resisted putting her thoughts on paper, but as the plan for her revenge began to gel, Evelyn realized her last work would be to prepare a manifesto detailing the harms that had been done to her and those who had become her closest and most intimate companions. She began with her ex-husband, spewing her hatred for him and frustration at his courtroom victory over several typed pages—what socialite she was sure he had fucked, what client she thought he had cheated, every malicious comment she had overheard him make about his friends. Evelyn hoped when the manifesto was published in the Fort Charles paper, which she would make certain happened, Miles Goodpasture's life would be as ruined as her own.

Evelyn lit a cigarette, inhaled deeply, and considered who should be next. There were so many people who had spit on her. Grinding out the half-finished smoke, Evelyn typed the name "Frank Martin." If it hadn't been for that private investigator Miles had hired, none of this would have happened. Evelyn had been shocked when her lawyer, Mark Lockridge, told her that Miles had concrete proof of her extracurricular activities. "You have to do something!" Evelyn had exclaimed. "It's not fair. Miles has done the same or worse."

"Evelyn, we've already had this conversation, more than once," her exasperated attorney had replied. "You only have your own suspicions. You don't have any surveillance. No one is willing to support your allegations with their own testimony. Miles is entitled to prove his case, and the judge is certainly going to allow Mr. Martin to testify. I don't see any way the films won't be admitted. I'll fight against it, of course, but I don't think we will be successful in excluding this evidence."

"Isn't there any way to keep that evidence out?" Evelyn pressed. "There has to be some way to prevent this."

"The only way this evidence would be excluded is if Frank Martin doesn't testify," Lockridge explained. "Since he's the person who made the surveillance, the rules of evidence require Martin's personal testimony as to when he made the films, how he conducted his surveillance, and so forth. But I don't see any legal basis on which to prevent Mr. Martin from being called as a witness for Miles."

Neither had Evelyn, but she hadn't been restricted to legal means. Tailing him had been easier than she had expected. She'd had a perfect shot that night, but as she sighted her target through the night scope on her long rifle, she'd been distracted by the headlights of a car coming down the gravel drive toward her hiding place. Her shot went low, missing her target's heart, allowing him to survive what had been intended as a fatal shot.

Evelyn chewed the nubs of what remained of her fingernails. All of her pain and humiliation could have been avoided, however, if that damn judge had listened to her attorney instead of siding with Miles and that prick Taylor Kitchens. It wouldn't have mattered what Miles had said or lied about. If the judge had not allowed the PI to testify, the ending would have been completely different. Evelyn knew all about Judge Kaufman and his famous wife, Allison Parker—storybook famous, featured in the local paper as the "golden couple." Evelyn ground her teeth thinking about the injustice. Maybe the judge and his wife wouldn't have a storybook life for much longer.

It was past midnight when Evelyn clicked the icon to power down her laptop. There were so many targets to consider, so many people who had harmed her. She had barely begun the list.

CHAPTER THIRTY-ONE

Maria Sanchez considered, with despair, the choices life had placed before her. *Not life,* she chided herself, *you. You, Maria Camila Luciana Sanchez, you have brought this day of reckoning. Life has nothing to do with it.* Would her life have been as terrible as this if she had acquiesced to her parents' wishes and married the man they had selected for her? Maria would never know, but she suspected nothing would have been as terrible as the situation in which she now found herself.

Sean McIntosh had saved her life, and that of her daughter, in more ways than one. Kind, generous, and a true gentleman, Sean had never pressed Maria for a physical relationship—not when he opened his home to her, not when he offered to help with Isabella, not when he deeded the title of the bodega to Maria. None of Sean's gifts or actions had strings attached.

Maria knew Sean loved her. Of that she had no doubt, but the detritus of her life and the burden of a handicapped child were more than Maria could ask Sean to assume. One day, she had thought when she left McIntosh Farms, Sean would understand that Maria had made the best decision for both of them. And how had she repaid Sean's love and generosity? With betrayal. Tears slid down Maria's face.

Tomorrow, she and Sean would make the drive to Cullman and Sacred Heart Monastery. Maria knew Sean would once again ask her to marry him, to allow him to make a home for her and Isabella. *It is the only way out,* Maria's fear whispered. *If you tell him about what you have done, you are lost. Even a man like Sean McIntosh will be unable to forgive such a betrayal.*

"*Buenos dias, Señora Sanchez.*" The screen door at the bodega's entrance creaked, announcing the arrival of a customer a second before the spoken greeting drew Maria's attention away from her thoughts. "*¿Cómo está?*"

"Jorge, how nice to see you." Maria made an unsuccessful attempt to wipe the teary evidence of despair from her face. "What brings you to my bodega today? Has Senor McIntosh sent you?" Maria busied herself rearranging a counter display. If she didn't face Jorge head-on, perhaps he would not notice her puffy eyes.

"Senor McIntosh has not sent me, senora," Jorge replied. In fact, Jorge wasn't sure why he had come to the bodega at all. He'd gone down to Gainesville earlier that morning to pick up some supplies for the farm. Stopping at the small bodega had not been on his agenda. But as he approached the turn off from the main highway to Bell, Maria Sanchez's image kept appearing at the corner of his eye. The image had become so vivid at one point that Jorge thought the woman had somehow materialized inside his vehicle. "You cannot escape the gift," the memory of his grandmother's voice reminded him. Obeying a command he did not understand, Jorge had turned the truck toward the bodega where he now found himself. "I think maybe I am looking for something here."

"I have fresh cilantro," Maria offered, "and vanilla beans from Mexico. I'll put your selection on Senor McIntosh's account. Just let me know when you've found what you need." Maria turned away, reluctant to make eye contact with Sean's employee, and began to rearrange canned goods in the back of the store.

Jorge was grateful to be ignored. Whatever he was supposed to find in the bodega, Jorge was fairly certain it would not be something he would see with his outer vision. A part of him felt like a fool. Jorge had never deliberately tried to use his gift. Would his feeble and untrained attempt even work? Closing his eyes, Jorge placed his hands on the wooden surface of the bodega's counter, polished smooth from years of use, opening his senses to the impressions left there by others.

At first, nothing unusual, just the *swish, swish* of the ceiling fan moving slowly above him and the clinking of tin as cans of vegetables and other goods were transferred from one shelf to another. In the distance, he could hear the muffled roar of vehicles as they passed by on the two-lane highway nearby. Willing his heart to slow and asking for his grandmother's guidance from across the veil, Jorge felt himself withdraw into himself, to a place he had never been. Releasing himself to the larger mystery, Jorge began to walk within the vision that appeared in his mind.

A woman was kneeling in front of a fire, her back turned toward him. Darkness and smoke filled the space around the woman, and the sound of weeping touched his ears. Although he had no sense of movement, Jorge found himself standing directly beside this woman. Now he could see what lay on the fire, and seeing, Jorge understood with horror the reason for the woman's anguish. A human heart lay burning on the pyre, the body from which it had been carved crumpled nearby, a body Jorge recognized.

"What have you done?" Jorge demanded of the kneeling woman. "What have you done?"

Maria Sanchez raised her head, dead eyes staring at Jorge. "The devil," she murmured, "the devil."

Jorge felt himself being pulled back, away from the woman, away from the burning heart, away from the body of Sean McIntosh. A new vision appeared. "*Abuela*," Jorge called to the shrouded figure of his dead grandmother. "*Abuela*, what does this mean?"

"You are called, my son. The gift has passed." A smile creased the crone's face, deepening the wrinkles that she wore as adornment. "This is the path you must walk."

"I don't know how to do this," Jorge exclaimed. "Is this the future? What am I to do? Who is the devil?"

Jorge's grandmother clasped the crucifix hanging from her neck. It was the same crucifix Jorge now wore, given to him by his *abuela* on her deathbed. "You will know him," she replied as she faded from Jorge's inner sight.

"Jorge, are you all right? Jorge, can you hear me?" The voice was insistent. As if in slow motion, Jorge allowed the world of the living to reclaim him. Gradually, it seemed, or maybe it was instantaneous—Jorge's sense of time seemed off to him—he felt the floor materialize beneath his feet. Cool air pushed from the slowly turning blades of the ceiling fan kissed Jorge's face. As if from a distance, Jorge heard Maria's worried voice and he struggled to emerge from wherever it was that he had been.

"I'm OK," he whispered. "At least I think I am." Jorge lowered himself to the bodega floor. "But I sure could use some water."

Maria rushed to the store room at the back of the bodega, pulled a glass from the shelf over a small sink, filled it with clear tap water, and hurried back to Jorge. "What happened to you?" she asked.

The water tasted good. Jorge sipped the cold liquid, uncertain of how to answer Maria's question. "I'm not sure." Jorge needed to process what he had seen and heard before he shared it with anyone, particularly someone who had been an actor in the disturbing scene that Jorge had visited. "Maybe I had a seizure."

"*Sí*, that is what it looked like," Maria agreed. "You were like stone. I called your name many times, but it seemed you could not hear."

"How long?" Jorge asked.

Taking the empty glass from Jorge's hand, Maria settled on the floor beside him. "Five minutes? Maybe ten?" Maria's furrowed brow spoke of her confusion. "I didn't realize anything was happening until I asked you a question and you didn't answer."

Maria felt Jorge's brow. "No fever, but your color is bad. I think you need to see a doctor."

Jorge shook his head in disagreement. The kind of doctor he needed wouldn't be found at the local hospital. "I'm OK, really," he assured Maria. "I'll sit here a few minutes more and then I'll be on my way."

It had taken some convincing to persuade Maria not to call for an ambulance or Jorge's boss. "No need to bother Senor McIntosh," Jorge insisted. "I'll swing by the twenty-four-hour clinic when I get back to Bell." Another glass of water and the return of healthy color to Jorge's face finally convinced Maria that he was fit to drive himself home.

The parking lot of the twenty-four-hour clinic was mostly empty when Jorge drove by forty-five minutes later. Not that it mattered. Jorge had no intention of seeking medical care for what he knew had been a spiritual experience. He waited until the day had quieted, when he knew he would not be interrupted by other ranch hands. Pulling a worn address book from the back of a dresser drawer, Jorge looked for the name of someone he had hoped never to need, and dialed the number he had hoped never to call.

"Hello," an ancient-sounding voice responded.

"It's Jorge. I need your help."

"Yes, the raven told me you would be calling," Miguel Santera replied. "She told me a vision would send you to me."

A chill ran its icy fingers up Jorge's spine. Miguel Santera, his great-uncle on his mother's side of the family, was a *brujo mayor*—a powerful witch and spell caster in the Brujería mystical traditions of Central and South America. "When the raven appears, your gift will manifest in its fullest power," Jorge remembered his grandmother's whispered message. "I need a spell," Jorge forced the words from his mouth.

"And why would a *curandero* want a spell from a *brujo*?" Santera asked. "*Curanderos* practice only white magic."

Jorge hesitated before asking, "Are you my *abuela*'s brother?"

"*Sí*." The *brujo*'s terse reply poured across the ether.

"Then you know why I am asking," Jorge replied quietly. "The blood of *curanderos* and *brujos* fill my veins. I did not ask for this burden, but I have accepted it."

"You tread on dangerous ground, my son," Santera warned. "White and black magic are a powerful combination. Many have tried to wield them together. Most have failed."

"Except for my *abuela*," Jorge stated what he hoped was true.

"Except for your *abuela*," Santera agreed, "but you are not your *abuela*."

"She told me years ago what I was, what I would become," Jorge replied. "I resisted. When she came in the vision today, I knew there was no escape."

A second silence filled the space between the two *brujos*. Finally, Jorge heard a sigh emanate from Santera. "What spell do you seek?"

"The most powerful one you have." Jorge hoped it would be enough. "I need to send the devil back to hell."

CHAPTER THIRTY-TWO

Plato McCall watched his quarry depart McIntosh Farms early Saturday morning. He had plenty left to do to make certain his plans for the evening would go off without interference, but Plato needed to see Sean leave his farm to confirm that the man was actually going to Cullman. Taking a backroad shortcut to the bodega, Plato pulled his car off the road, parking it behind an abandoned shed, and waited. He did not have to surveil very long. "Adios, fucker," Plato called as Sean's truck passed by a few minutes later, Maria Sanchez's face silhouetted in the passenger side window.

Plato had time to kill. Having calculated McIntosh's travel time to and from the monastery in Cullman, Plato knew he had hours before he would need to set up at Sean's house. The sun would have set well before Plato needed to break into the ranch. Still, he'd need to assure himself that none of the ranch hands had stayed past regular working hours. Collateral damage was such a pain in the ass.

Back at his house, Plato began to assemble the tools he would need for the night's task. If Sean McIntosh had a security system in his home, Plato figured he'd need to construct an electronic bypass before he entered the house. Plato wanted to be inside the ranch house well before Sean returned with Maria and her child. *Being in the big house had some benefits,* Plato reflected wryly. One of his cell mates had taught him the basics about home security systems. *If people only knew how easy it was to disable the systems they'd paid big bucks for.* Plato grinned as he double-checked the electronic devices he would use if he needed to disarm Sean's alarms. False security was no security—something Sean McIntosh would soon discover.

Satisfied that he could access the ranch house without alerting the alarm company or police, Plato laid out the more individual tools he had assembled for the night's foray: gun, pliers, rope, blindfolds, cloths to fashion into gags—the only person he wanted to hear screaming was his target—a propane torch, a blade. Handling the kid would be tricky. Plato needed to inflict enough damage to get Sean's attention, to make him do what he wanted, but not enough to kill the kid outright. That would come later.

⋇⟞⟝⋇

"Good afternoon, sister," Sean McIntosh greeted the nun who had responded when he rang the bell at the monastery's gate. "We are here to see Mother Superior."

"Mother is expecting you," the nun replied, eyes cast at Sean's feet rather than at his face. "Follow me, please."

The grounds of Sacred Heart Monastery were beautiful. Encompassing several acres of wooded and landscaped nature, the Benedictine sisters had built over the years a chapel, adorned with stained glass from Germany, an academy for educating the children of Cullman and close-lying communities, and a retreat center. Nestled in a copse near the chapel stood the convent itself, and it was to this building of moderate size that Sean and Maria were led by their guide.

A small vestibule with two straight-back chairs greeted the trio as they entered. "Wait here," the nun instructed. Sean and Maria watched the nun disappear into what they presumed was mother superior's office. "I can see why they call the rooms where the nuns live 'cells,'" Maria remarked, peering down the narrow hallway. "Those doors can't be more than ten feet apart. The rooms they open into have to be tiny."

"They take vows of poverty," Sean reminded Maria. "I guess where they sleep doesn't make much difference to someone who has chosen a religious life."

Maria paced. Her heart raced. *Will she know me?* Maria worried that her daughter would not want to be separated from these women in long black robes who had been her caregivers for most of Isabella's short life. Out loud she said, "I'm scared."

Sean wrapped his arms around Maria, pulling her to his chest, and resting his chin on her dark hair. "There is nothing to be afraid of, *a grhá*. Isabella knows you, she knows you are her mother."

"But this is all she has known," Maria fretted.

"It is true this is all she has known," a strong voice agreed, "but because she has known love and safety, she will have no trouble adjusting to the love and safety you will provide as her mother."

"Sister Angelina." Sean nodded in the mother superior's direction. "I have told Maria much the same. We are both grateful for the home that you and the sisters have provided Isabella. I have assured Maria that Isabella will adjust quickly to life in the world and that there is nothing to worry about."

The nun reached for Maria, drawing her toward her. "My child, your daughter has been a gift for all of us at Sacred Heart. Thank you for sharing her with us these last four years. But it is time for her to return to you, to her mother. We have prayed for this reconciliation, and the Lord has shown us that this is the time. Place your trust in Him, my child, and all will be well."

Maria bowed her head, accepting the nun's words. "Give me your blessing, Mother," she whispered. "That I may be worthy."

The mother superior spoke softly in Maria's ear, made the sign of the cross on Maria's forehead, and asked, "Are you ready to see Isabella?"

"It will be dark soon," Allison called to her husband. "We need to head back to the marina."

Jim Kaufman waved his acknowledgment and turned the ski boat to starboard. Stretching her fit frame across the leather bench at the back of the boat, Allison closed her eyes and accepted the sun's late-afternoon caress. The day had been perfect. Charlotte and Mack had each brought a friend for an afternoon of skiing and rafting. Completely worn out, all four children now lay napping in the boat's forward cabin. Too much sun, too much fun, and too much fried chicken had proved more than their small bodies could handle. *These are the kinds of days I will remember when I am an old woman*, Allison thought as she watched her husband steer the boat toward shore. *And how lucky am I?* she asked, gazing at the strong and still-virile man she had married so many years earlier. *What would my life be without him?*

"Better wake the kiddos," Jim's voice interrupted Allison's thoughts. "We'll be docking in five."

Allison pulled herself to a sitting position, yawned, and accepted the inevitable end to a family day on the reservoir. Life was good.

CHAPTER
THIRTY-THREE

The waste overflowing from the trash basket by the side of Frank Martin's desk this Saturday morning resembled an avant-garde depiction of an erupting volcano. Wads of yellow, crumpled-up paper torn from the legal pad lying on Frank's desk, a couple of empty Burger King bags, two foul-smelling foam coffee containers stained dark brown, and an unknown number of discarded cigar butts—Frank barely noticed the detritus that cluttered his office floor as he tossed yet another pulverized cigar in the general direction of the wire waste container. Once, one of Frank's clients had been foolish enough to comment on the assorted clutter decorating the PI's office. Frank's rapt attention while the client preached about the merits of a clean work space had been misinterpreted by the vigilante as acquiescence to his message.

"Thank you," Frank had replied after his client finally stopped telling Frank how to clean up his office. "I've got something to show you." Rising from his desk, Frank led the client from his office, down the hallway to the office's reception area, shook the man's hand, and said, "Don't let the door hit you in the ass on the way out. I'll send you a check next week for the balance of your retainer."

Flabbergasted, the client replied, "Wha—wha—what do you mean?"

"I'm firing you," Frank replied, shoving the surprised man out the door. "I don't tell you how to run your business, and you don't tell me how to run mine."

News of Frank's actions had spread quickly through Fort Charles, but rather than hurting the PI's reputation as his irate client had hoped, Frank's irascibility enhanced his already-colorful persona. In truth, Frank's office never got too bad. A cleaning service came weekly on Sunday afternoons, so while Frank's office might resemble disaster zone by the end of the week, Mondays offered Frank a clean canvas on which to mimic a Mondrian or de Kooning.

Frank swiveled his leather chair away from his desk to face the ancient wooden credenza where a battered Mr. Coffee brewed a fresh pot of Joe. Seeing the brew light switch from red to green, Frank retrieved the glass pot and poured. Holding the steaming mug with both hands, Frank leaned back in his chair and let his newest theory flit through his mind. The events of the night he was shot were still a mystery to Frank. Dr. Lopez said he might never recover his memory of what happened to him; then again, he might. Operating on the assumption that his memory would never return, Frank had turned his considerable investigative skills to discovering the identity of his attacker.

Frank reviewed all the case files that had been open at the time of the shooting. Originally, both the sheriff and Allison thought that the most likely candidate for the bad guy had to be Sean McIntosh, but the more Frank had thought about the case and evaluated the information that had been subsequently uncovered, the less inclined Frank was to think that the shooter was his cousin. However, that didn't mean the shooter wasn't somehow connected to Sean—either hired by him or going after the rancher.

The time Frank had spent at McIntosh Farms convinced Frank that his cousin was innocent, at least of trying to have Frank killed. He still wasn't convinced that Sean was telling him all the truth, but Frank's gut told him that whatever it was that Sean was hiding, in all likelihood it wasn't related to whoever had tried to kill him. Or was it? Just when Frank would convince himself that Sean McIntosh and the theft of Blue Scarlet weren't connected to the attempt on Frank's life, a little nudge would cause Frank to question his judgment. Frank hoped that the trip he and Allison planned to take on Monday would clarify things for him. Allison was the right person to talk to the woman who owned the bodega. Frank was sure of that. By Monday evening, Frank figured he'd have an answer to the remaining questions he had about Sean McIntosh.

Frank's newest theory, however, on the identity of the shooter had taken an unexpected turn, and it was this theory that had brought Frank to his office on a Saturday morning. If Sean McIntosh was not involved in the attempt on Frank's life, who would have had a reason to see him dead? Mulling the question in his head, Frank reached into the sack of chocolate-glazed doughnuts he had bought at the Krispy Kreme drive-through on his way to the office. The sickly aroma of sugar wafted from the open bag as Frank searched for just one more of the delights on Dr. Lopez's forbidden list. Sugar always helped Frank think, or so he told himself as he demolished the last doughnut, wadded the empty sack, and tossed it on the pile of trash surrounding the mini Mount Vesuvius.

Frank poured another cup of coffee before pulling the legal pad toward him and writing, *Potential shooters: Evelyn Goodpasture's lovers. Pierre Chastain, Dwight England, Pete Hubbard.* Frank had considered and then discarded Mavis Johnson and Evelyn Goodpasture as suspects. Neither woman fit the profile of a female killer. Furthermore, if Mavis Johnson had made the attempt on Frank's life, he thought she would have confessed in a suicide note. Frank knew from talking to Toby that no such confession had been found.

It had taken a while for Frank to consider Evelyn's sex partners are possible suspects. After all, he was shot at well before he testified at Evelyn's trial. However, Frank knew that Mark Lockridge would have told Evelyn about Frank's upcoming testimony as soon as Frank's report had been produced by the other side during discovery, and if Evelyn had given her lovers a heads-up on being outed in court, that could put an entirely different light on the subject.

Frank didn't think much of England or Hubbard as suspects. *Hell, the men advertised themselves as sex partners on the Internet,* Frank thought. But Chastain was another matter. *Look what happened to Pierre Chastain,* Frank reflected. *Fired and run out of town. Basically unemployable in his field.* Yes, Pierre Chastain had a substantial motivation for keeping Frank's testimony out of court. But was it enough to make Chastain try to kill him? Maybe. Frank had seen people killed for lesser reasons.

Sean McIntosh or someone connected to him? Or Pierre Chastain? Once again, Frank wavered on the suspect he found most suspicious. Frank perused his notes searching for an answer. Who knew he was going out to the old Anderson place the night he was shot? The answer to that question had to be Sean. According to his cousin, Frank had insisted on going to the meeting with the man who had identified himself as Blue Scarlet's kidnapper, or more accurately, Blue Scarlet's horsenapper. Sean had received a call earlier that day, instructing him to bring $100,000 in cash to the Anderson place. Under no circumstances was Sean to contact the sheriff. Failure to comply with the horsenapper's instructions would result in Blue Scarlet's death. Sean had argued with Frank, insisting that the instructions be followed to the letter, but Frank had convinced Sean that dealing with these types of situations was exactly why Sean had hired him. Moreover, Frank had no intention of taking real money to the meet. Kidnapping and extortion was a far cry from murder in Frank's book. Or at least it used to be. Chomping on the nasty end of his cigar, Frank sent a silent "Thank you" to whoever might be listening. Next time, he wouldn't make the same mistake.

Frank wished the pieces of the puzzle would magically fit together, but to his continuing frustration, the puzzle seemed more confusing than ever. After the Anderson place fiasco, Sean had gotten a call from the horsenapper claiming that Blue Scarlet had been killed, and telling Sean he would be next. It was completely possible that the attempt on Frank's life had been made by the horsenapper when he confronted Frank and discovered that Frank had brought only part of the ransom money. Or, maybe the horsenapper shot Frank in a fit of rage because Sean had sent Frank instead of coming himself. If only he could retrieve just a portion of that night's events, Frank knew he would have a better idea of what had happened to him, and why.

The more Frank thought about why he had gone to the Anderson place to begin with, the less viable Pierre Chastain became as a suspect. *How would Pierre even have known where I was going to be the night I got shot?* Frank mused. Pierre Chastain didn't fit the profile for a stalker, and that was the only way Frank figured Pierre would have ended up as the shooter—the man would have actually had to follow Frank from his office to the Anderson place. Besides that, Frank considered, what were the odds that Chastain would be stalking him the same night that Frank was meeting Blue Scarlet's horsenapper? No; the odds were too great. No one had that sort of luck.

Frank grimaced at the taste of cold, stale coffee as he absentmindedly took a swig. "Blech," he muttered, pouring the remains into the Mr. Coffee pot behind him. Swishing the dark liquid around and around with a twist of his wrist, Frank poured a portion of what he hoped was now lukewarm caffeine back into the waiting mug. A quick glance into the Krispy Kreme bag confirmed Frank's worst fear. All of the doughnuts were gone. "Well, crap," Frank announced. How was he supposed to drink his coffee without a doughnut? Stacking the case files in an amazingly neat pile, Frank heaved himself from the desk chair and headed for the door. He'd made as much progress today as he thought possible. Past experience told Frank he'd do well to let his competing theories war it out in his subconscious for a day or two longer. The answer would come to him. He'd get Allison's take on all of it on the ride to Bell on Monday.

CHAPTER THIRTY-FOUR

Sunday dawned cool and overcast, an anomaly for this time of the year in north Florida. Rubbing sleep from his eyes, Jorge studied the objects he had placed on the coffee table in his small apartment just a few hours before. Working for Sean McIntosh, and being paid a decent wage, had allowed Jorge to save enough money to buy half of a duplex in a decent area of Bell. Given the magic he was going to attempt, Jorge was thankful that his next-door neighbor had taken a weekend trip to the coast. If anything went wrong, no one other than himself would suffer.

Miguel Santera had cautioned Jorge against the action he now contemplated. "You are untested," the *brujo* had warned. "*Brujo* magic is powerful, more powerful than *curandero* magic, and you have welded neither. What you attempt is suicide."

"I intend no disrespect," Jorge had replied, "but I cannot ignore what the spirits have shown me, no more than can I ignore my *abuela*'s words. Senor McIntosh is in danger. I must discover who the devil is"—Jorge had paused as he considered the seriousness of his next words—"and then I must send him back to hell."

Now, heeding the brujo's warning, Jorge readied himself for the ritual he needed to perform. First, he would purify himself and the space. Striking a match, Jorge carefully lit the fat, wrapped sage stick. When the sage had blazed sufficiently, Jorge extinguished the flame and allowed the resulting smoke to waft about him. Waving the smoking sage across his body, then over and around the coffee table where the implements of magic were displayed, Jorge beseeched the guardians of *curandero* magic to surround and protect him. "*Abuela*," he intoned, "I seek your protection and that of our ancestors. I call upon the light to shine upon the darkness, to expose the demon who poses in human form."

A light breeze caressed Jorge's cheek, drawing his attention to the raven's feather placed nearest to him on the table. Unaided by visible means, the black feather rose a few inches above the tabletop and began to move in a circular fashion. "Oh, Raven Spirit, Master Magician and keeper of secrets, illuminate my path. Reveal the darkness. Protect me from evil. Transform my magic for the greater good." Jorge began to shiver as he felt a cold presence descend on him. "I submit myself to the magic of the *curanderos*, and I invoke the power of the *brujos*." Jorge closed his eyes to the physical world, and opened himself to the invisible one. "I claim my inheritance," he asserted with conviction. "I am *curandero*. I am *brujo*. The magic of mystical union is mine."

Pain erupted in Jorge's head, and he felt, rather than saw, a blinding flash of brilliant light fill the small room. Sweat began to pour from his forehead, while the rest of his body continued to shake with biting cold. Then, from a distance, an image began to form before him. Jorge strained to discern the shadowy figure which seemed somehow familiar to him. His *abuela* had said he would know the devil, and it was this familiarity that now pulled at the edges of his conscious mind. A man. Jorge was certain the figure was male, but the figure's face continued to be obscured. Pushing through pain that seemed intolerable, Jorge demanded, "By the power of the *brujos*, show yourself, Demon."

The figure turned toward Jorge, replying to his command with a sinister laugh. "You are too late."

⊷⊶

Tick. Tick. Tick. An annoying sound picked at Jorge. *Tick. Tick. Tick. So far away,* Jorge thought. *Not important. Tick. Tick. Tick.* The sound increased in intensity, reaching into the fog that held Jorge in a tight embrace. Louder now. *Tick. Tick. Tick.* Insistent. Unremitting. The sound scratched its way into Jorge's shroud, inflicting small pains as it touched Jorge's skin, urging him to return.

"*¡Mierda!*" Jorge exclaimed, reaching for the knife he was certain someone had impaled in his head. The slightest change in position was excruciating. Slowly, Jorge realized he was lying on the floor of his living room, the implements he had placed on the coffee table the night before scattered nearby. Jorge pushed himself to a sitting position. *Tick. Tick. Tick.* The sound of the old-fashioned clock on a nearby table roused Jorge to full awareness, bringing into sharp focus the memory of the preceding night's events.

Fighting through the pain, Jorge forced himself from the floor. His magic had revealed the danger. Sending another prayer to the spirits of his ancestors, Jorge grabbed the keys to his truck and ran from the house. Then, reflecting on the power of the Madonna, Jorge pleaded, "Help me."

CHAPTER THIRTY-FIVE

"Be sure and call Sharon if you can't get home by five today," Allison reminded her husband. "I have no idea when Frank and I will be finished in Bell, but with a four-hour drive, you shouldn't expect us until well after supper, maybe even as late as ten o'clock."

Jim adjusted the blue-and-yellow-striped tie he had looped around the white oxford dress shirt that hugged his slim physique. "I don't know why I bother," he grumbled. "I could be wearing jeans and a T-shirt under my robe and no one would know the difference." Giving the constricting silk a final tug, Jim replied to his wife's reminder. "Not a problem.

The only items on my docket today are some motion hearings set for this morning and early afternoon. I thought you and Frank were going to stay in Bell overnight. Change of plans?"

"An overnight is still a possibility," Allison admitted, "but neither of us really wants to stay over. It just depends on how long we spend at the bodega."

"Did you ever find out that woman's name?" Jim pulled a navy blazer from its hanger.

"Actually Toby did some digging for us. Her name is Maria Sanchez. She's listed as the bodega's owner on the Gilchrist County property records." Allison turned off the bathroom light and followed her husband into the couple's bedroom. "Toby called the sheriff down there, had him run a quiet check on her."

"And?" Jim prompted.

"Clean as far as any criminal record or run-ins with the constabulary," Allison answered. "But here's the interesting part: not only did the sheriff down there confirm what Frank had been told about the woman living at Sean McIntosh's ranch for a while, he told Toby that Maria Sanchez had a baby while she was living with McIntosh. The gossip all over Bell at the time was that the kid was Sean's bastard."

Jim whistled softly. "Well, if that rumor is true—I mean, about the kid's parentage—I can see why Sean refrained from sharing that small detail with

Frank. It would also explain why Sean allegedly paid for the bodega the Sanchez woman owns."

Following her husband down the hall to the kitchen, Allison continued. "All that makes sense except for one thing."

"Which is?" Jim nudged.

"There's no record of any baby being born to Maria Sanchez at the ranch, in a hospital, or anywhere else." Allison peered into the open refrigerator, grabbed a yogurt cup, peeled the lid, and continued. "If a baby was born, why would there not be a record of the birth? If the kid was Sean's, that doesn't mean he'd necessarily be listed on the birth certificate."

"That's true," Jim agreed. "Happens more than people realize. State law only requires the mother's name on the birth certificate."

"Right." Allison poured a cup of coffee to go with her yogurt. Settling into a chair at the large wooden kitchen table, Allison considered the implications of her husband's comment while she quickly demolished what she considered to be a pitifully small breakfast. *If Sean's name on the birth certificate wasn't the issue, what was?* "All I can figure is the Sanchez woman didn't want a record of the birth, assuming there really was a baby. After all, the Gilchrist County sheriff said most of what he had heard about a baby was rumor."

"Sounds like a typical small town," Jim remarked, "and potential fodder for a good novel, but how does any of this relate to Frank's investigation? Have I missed something?"

Allison poured the remains of her coffee into a to-go cup, topped it off with fresh caffeine, and tossed the remnants of her breakfast into the trash. Gathering her briefcase, Allison paused to answer her husband's question. "Frank thinks the theft of Blue Scarlet was an inside job. He's cleared all the ranch hands. The only other person who had access to and inside knowledge about the workings of the ranch would have been Maria Sanchez. Frank is suspicious because Sean never mentioned the woman in any context. So, you know Frank, he's determined to interrogate Maria—or more accurately, have me interrogate her—to see if he can make a connection between her and the theft."

Jim placed a kiss on his wife's forehead. "Be careful, hon. If the woman's involved in the theft of that horse, she may be involved in the attempt on Frank's life." Worry marred Jim's handsome face. "Too many unknowns. This trip has the potential to be a lot more dangerous than I thought it was going to be."

"You worry too much." Allison gave her husband's cheek a gentle caress. "We'll talk to the Sanchez woman, find out what we can, then head back. It'll be fine."

Jim's retort was interrupted by the loud entrance of the couple's children. "Mama, can I go to the stables today? Jeri wants to work with me before the next show." Charlotte smiled, willing an affirmative answer. "Sharon can drop me off, and Daddy can pick me up. Please?"

"That's not fair." Mack pouted. "She gets to do special stuff all the time."

"Come on, you two." Allison laughed. "Be nice to each other. Charlotte, it's fine with me so long as your father agrees. Mack"—Allison ruffled her son's unruly hair—"we'll set up something special for you next weekend."

Gathering her purse and briefcase, Allison gave her husband a quick kiss on her way to the garage. "Love you, all of you," she reminded her family. "See you tonight."

Driving the short distance to town, Allison reflected on the morning's events and hoped that some semblance of sibling peace had been restored between her children. Charlotte would spend the afternoon at Overlook Riding Club training Diamond Girl for the upcoming dressage event scheduled for Atlanta around Labor Day. Saturday, Mack would get an afternoon at the movies with two of his friends. Allison hoped her children would remain friends throughout their lives. The years Allison had spent estranged from her brother, Rice, had been difficult, both for her and for her brother. Although they were now reconciled, the events that had led to that reconciliation had been terrible. Allison offered a silent prayer, gratitude for her children's lives and a hope for their continued goodwill toward each other. Life was difficult. Family was important.

Allison pulled her Miata into the first empty space next to the building that housed Parker & Jackson and the offices of Martin Investigations. As usual, Donna Pevey had beaten her to the office. "I like to get the coffee going, make sure everything's where it should be before you and David get here," Donna had explained when Allison questioned the need for such an early arrival. "Makes me twitchy otherwise." Allison hadn't argued. Parker & Jackson ran smoothly, in no small part because of Donna's eccentricities and obsessive-compulsive tendencies.

Entering through the employee entrance, Allison inhaled the aroma of the morning's fresh brew. "Hey, Donna, it's me," Allison called out. "Have you heard from Frank this morning?"

Donna stood in the hallway outside Allison's office, her hands full of legal files. "You just missed his call. Said he'll be here by eight fifteen and ready to hit the road. Is there anything you need from me before you leave?"

"I think I'm good," Allison replied. "I'm just grabbing a couple of extra legal pads. Everything else is in my car, and I'll get it on the way out."

"Is your cell the best way to reach you if I need to today?" Donna asked.

"Should be." Allison nodded. "We might swing by McIntosh Farms on the way out of town. Just depends on how long we spend talking to Maria Sanchez. I'll have my phone on wherever we are."

A loud car horn announced Frank's arrival. "I don't expect any calls today, though, and with David on vacation, the office ought to be pretty quiet," Allison observed. "If things are slow, why don't you head out early and just let the answering service field any calls?"

Donna considered her boss's suggestion. "Thanks, Allison. I might do just that."

Grabbing two legal pads from her secretary's desk, Allison headed for the door. "See you tomorrow. If we get in late tonight, don't expect me until midmorning."

CHAPTER THIRTY-SIX

E velyn Goodpasture stared at the haggard woman in the bathroom mirror. Shaggy, unkempt, and greasy hair hung limply around her face. Evelyn had lost so much weight after the divorce that she now appeared skeletal. Deep, dark circles accentuated the lines under her blue eyes. High cheekbones, one of the few physical attributes that had given Evelyn a semblance of beauty in her younger days, now crowned cavernous valleys on either side of her mouth. And her mouth—all that remained was a thin, dry, cracked scab across her face.

The woman in the mirror sneered. *What difference do your looks make now? All the better to be invisible.*

No one cares about ugly. Evelyn pulled a thin comb through her even thinner hair. To her dismay, a clump of gray hair filled the comb's teeth. How had she come to this?

If she went through with her plans, if she was successful, Evelyn knew her looks would no longer matter. She would either be dead or headed to the penitentiary. Evelyn doubted that death-row inmates got makeovers.

She was so tired, though. Retribution and revenge had been Evelyn's constant and sole companions since her divorce trial a few months earlier. The need for nourishment and cleanliness had gradually diminished. Fueled by an anger she had not known she was capable of possessing, Evelyn had schemed, plotted, and visualized the violence of her bullets as the soft bodies of her victims were blown apart. How odd, she had thought, the first time her murderous fantasy had culminated in an orgasmic release. Was this how serial killers were born?

Evelyn's weapons lay across her bed. Picking up the GLOCK .19, Evelyn pressed the end of the shiny, black barrel against her temple. *Why not just end it now?* Returning the gun to its resting place with the others, Evelyn argued with the silent voice that had intruded more and more often into her thoughts these days. *No, not yet. Afterward. Then I can rest.*

Her hand moved as if it were a living being, separate from Evelyn's own will power. Slowly, Evelyn picked up the handgun. The metal barrel felt like ice. Was this the coldness of the grave? *It will be over in a second,* the words formed in her mind. *All you have to do is pull the trigger.*

An anguished scream shook Evelyn as she threw the GLOCK across the bedroom. "No!" she wailed, covering her ears with her hands and falling to her knees. Evelyn pounded the floor with her fists, the concentrated violence ripping open the woman's knuckles. Blood dripped from the wounds, staining the beige carpet. Evelyn began to heave—tears of regret, pain, and retribution mixed together—washing her free, clearing her mind, returning her sanity.

Soon, she told herself. *Soon.*

CHAPTER THIRTY-SEVEN

Sean McIntosh strained against the ropes that held him prisoner. Cautiously, keeping his bowed head against his chest, Sean tried to open eyes that he feared were so swollen that his attempt might be for naught. The last beating had been severe. Given the pain that burned through his chest with each breath, Sean was pretty certain that one or more of his ribs had been broken. He hurt like a motherfucker, but as long as his lungs weren't punctured, he had a chance if he could just get loose.

His tormenter wasn't in the room, of that Sean was certain. The only sound was his own labored breathing. Thank God he could still see, although

poorly and only with his left eye; the right one refused to cooperate. Sean didn't know whether he
had been permanently blinded or whether the eye
was glued shut with blood. He'd deal with that later
when he got out of this mess; if he got out was a scenario Sean pushed from his mind.

Maria. Maria and Isabella—what had happened
to them? Had their captor hurt them? Sean struggled to pull his hand from the bindings. "Shit!" he
cursed. No matter how hard he pulled, the ropes
refused to loosen. Taking a painful breath, Sean
commanded himself to review the events of the past
hours. Maybe there would be a clue somewhere,
something that would help him, that would save the
three of them, or if not him, something that would
save Maria and her child.

Their captor had taken Sean by surprise. The
last thing Sean remembered before waking tied to
the chair where he now found himself was unlock-
ing the door of his house and walking into the front
hallway. From the dull throbbing in the back on his
head, Sean figured the man who attacked him had
used a heavy object to knock him unconscious. If the
wound had been severe enough to bleed, enough
time had passed for coagulation to have occurred.
Sean couldn't feel any warm liquid running down
the back of his neck. A concussion was assured but
maybe just a mild one.

The man who had stood facing Sean when he regained consciousness the night before had seemed familiar, but Sean hadn't been able to place him right off. "Who are you?" Sean had asked. "What do you want?"

"You don't remember me?" the man had seemed surprised or disappointed. "After what you did to me? Maybe this will help you remember," he added, delivering what was to become the first of many punishing blows to Sean's face. "Boston. Twelve years ago. You should have minded your own business."

Recognition crossed Sean's face. "You were trying to kidnap your sister."

"That's right," the man spit. "You cost me ten years of my life." Another flurry of blows rained pain on Sean's face and head. "And now, it's payback."

Sean had passed in and out of consciousness for hours, each time his awakening being followed by a torment of verbal, mental, and physical abuse from the man who had eventually identified himself as Plato McCall. Sean's demands about the whereabouts of Maria and her child had been met with sneers and further punishment.

Now, lifting his head and gazing through his one good eye, Sean examined the room that had become his prison. Light filtered through the shades that were closed against the front windows, telling Sean that the night had passed. The ranch's regular employees wouldn't come up to the house. They had assigned jobs and were used to not seeing Sean for days at a time. No one would think askance at his absence nor question his whereabouts. No one would look for Maria either. Sean had instructed her to leave a sign on the bodega door, telling customers she planned to be out of town for a few days. Salvation, if it came in time, would be by his own hands. The sound of footsteps caught Sean's attention. More than one person was coming down the hallway toward the room where he was bound.

"Bitch, you better do as I say," Sean heard the anger in Plato McCall's voice.

"When have I not obeyed you?" Maria's plaintive reply assured Sean that she was still alive but confused him as well. Did Maria know McCall? What did she mean about obeying him?

Abruptly, the door to the room was thrust open. Stumbling, Maria Sanchez fell across the doorway, catching herself before she hit the floor. Her hair was disheveled and her dress torn at the shoulder. As far as Sean could tell, Maria was physically unharmed. "Maria," he called out, "are you all right?" Glaring at McCall, Sean growled, "If you've hurt her, I'll kill you."

Plato McCall laughed. "More likely, I'll be the one doing the killing." Reaching down to grab Maria's hair, McCall yanked the kneeling woman to her feet. "Shut up, bitch," he ordered in response to Maria's cry of pain. "Shut the fuck up until I tell you to speak."

"Leave her alone!" Sean yelled. "I'm the one who sent you to prison. She's nothing to you."

Plato McCall shoved Maria toward one of the room's other chairs. "You're right, of course," he replied. "She's nothing to me. But the same can't be said of you, now, can it?"

Sean refused McCall's bait, keeping silent.

"So that's how you want to play it?" McCall asked. "Very well. Let's start with how this bitch has deceived you. Then we'll see how much she means to you." Slapping Maria across the face, McCall smiled. "Tell him about Blue Scarlet, Maria." Tears began to roll down the beautiful woman's face. "Tell him," McCall demanded again. "Tell him or I'll get the child."

Sean watched the tableau unfold before him. He knew what Maria would tell him before she uttered the words. "It's all right, Maria. Whatever you did, it doesn't matter to me," Sean assured the woman.

"He told me he would hurt Isabella," Maria whispered the excuse for her betrayal. "That he knew where she was, and if I did not help him take the horse, he would hurt my child." Maria's tears began to fall in earnest. Sobbing, she petitioned, "Forgive me, Sean."

Rage filled Sean McIntosh's brain. He would kill Plato McCall. He didn't know how, but by God, he would kill the man, the lowest form of life, a man who would threaten to harm an innocent child. Raising his chin in a gesture of defiance, Sean re-marked, "You a pedophile, McCall? Can't think of another reason you'd go after a child." Darkness came quickly, close on the heels of blinding pain. Sean felt a smile cross his face before his awareness fled.

CHAPTER THIRTY-EIGHT

"Did you tell Sean we'd be in town today?" Allison was curious.

"Nah. He'd want to know why, and I don't think he knows that I've discovered Maria Sanchez," Frank replied, turning his attention from the two-lane road to answer his traveling companion. "I was afraid he'd think something was up, maybe give the woman advance warning."

Allison gazed contentedly at the green and verdant pastureland that surrounded the strip of state highway on which Frank's big truck was easily cruising. It had turned out to be a perfect day for a road trip. "If Sean has been intentionally hiding his relationship with the Sanchez woman from you—or anyone else for that matter—I would bet you a cold one that he's already warned Maria about you." Allison leaned her head against the passenger side window, soaking in the gentle rays of morning sunshine. "How much farther?"

"Not far." Frank glanced at the map displayed on the truck's dashboard GPS. "Looks like our arrival time is fifteen minutes away."

"I talked to Jim about this case over the weekend, thought maybe another perspective would give me some insight into what kind of relationship there might be or used to be between Sean and Maria." Allison reached into the briefcase resting against her feet and pulled out a legal pad. "Jim made some interesting observations. I've jotted them down in no particular order. Want to hear them?"

"Sure." Frank's reply was unnecessary, just as Allison's last question was rhetorical.

"First, maybe Maria has something on Sean, something damaging or illegal," Allison began. "Sean wouldn't want us to know about Maria because she might spill the beans on him."

"No offense to the judge, but that's ridiculous." Frank snorted.

"Jim thought so, too," Allison replied, "but I asked him to think of every possibility, and that is certainly one of them, however remote."

"Yeah, true," Frank admitted. "What else did Jim come up with?"

"Obviously the one we've already considered—that Sean and Maria had a child together, and Sean set her up at the bodega to get rid of a problem—Maria, not the kid. No one admits to even seeing a child at the ranch, so maybe there never was one. Maybe there *was* a relationship, it ended, and for some reason, Sean gave Maria enough money to get set up on her own." Allison gazed out the truck window. "Some of that fits; some of it doesn't."

"What part of that theory feels right to you?" Frank trusted Allison's intuition. He couldn't explain how it worked, but his companion had been dead on the money more than once.

"Sean McIntosh seems an honorable man to me. If Maria lived at the ranch for a while, and all our intel points to that allegation as being true, then she was there either because she had a problem that Sean was trying to help her with or because Sean had feelings for her." Allison frowned. She wasn't explaining this right. "I know I'm missing something, but it's just beyond my grasp."

Frank knew Allison would work the problem until the answer came to her. He was curious to know if there were any other theories he and Allison had not considered. "Did the judge have any other thoughts?"

"Jim said if the theft of Blue Scarlet was an inside job, there had to be enough of a payback for someone to risk helping whoever took the horse. I told him we'd satisfied ourselves that none of the hired hands were involved, and that only left Maria Sanchez as a person with knowledge of the ranch and its security systems." Allison flipped through her notes. "So, Jim asked me, what would make Maria Sanchez help a horse thief?"

Frank moved uncomfortably in the driver's seat. The answer seemed obvious now that he and Allison asked the right question. "You thinking what I'm thinking?"

Allison nodded. "The child. That's the wild card in this. There has to be a child somewhere, either still alive or dead under dire circumstances."

"My bet is alive," Frank interrupted. "You would do anything to protect Charlotte and Mack."

"And so would any mother who loved her child," Allison finished Frank's sentence.

Further conversation ceased when the tinny female voice from the GPS advised, "Your destination is ahead, on left." Heeding the directive, Frank pulled the truck into a deserted parking lot adjacent to the small building that housed Maria Sanchez's bodega.

"I don't like the look of this," Frank muttered, reaching under the driver's seat for the gun he carried there. "Stay in the car while I check this out."

"Not a chance," Allison replied, pulling her GLOCK from her purse and opening the passenger side door.

The pair approached the bodega carefully, keeping to the side of the small structure and away from the front windows and door. Motioning for Allison to get behind him, Frank lifted a booted foot to the low porch and crouched below the nearest window.

"Frank," Allison hissed, "look at the door. There's a note of some kind stuck between the door and the jamb."

Frank raised his head slowly and looked through the store's window. Convinced that no one was inside waiting to shoot him, Frank stood with a groan and walked over to retrieve the white paper. "It says the bodega will be closed until the fifteenth. That's today." Frank handed the paper to Allison. "Looks like water marks on the exposed edges, too, maybe from a blowing rain? This note's been here for a couple of days."

"There's nothing odd about the shop being closed for a few days," Allison reflected, "but I wonder why Maria isn't here now? The note says she'll be open for business today."

"I guess we'll be making a stop at Sean's place after all." Frank headed toward his truck. "Sean needs to get straight with us about Maria Sanchez."

CHAPTER THIRTY-NINE

S ean McIntosh's ranch house rested on a small knoll, giving its residents a commanding view of the main approach to the house from the state highway, as well as to the paddocks, barns, and other outbuildings that sprawled across the acreage closest to the main dwelling. With binoculars, which Jorge now held against his eyes, one could see the cars and trucks that sat parked in various areas, most notably down by the barn and ranch bunkhouse. Closer to the main house, Jorge noticed two other vehicles. The Land Rover parked in front of the house belonged to his boss. The other, a black van with darkened windows, sat partially hidden behind a grove of palms and landscape grasses off to the left side of the ranch-style home. *A fitting car for the devil.* Jorge lowered the binoculars and assessed the situation that lay before him.

He needed to be as close as possible to effectively work the spell he planned to use. If the van was unlocked and he could obtain a personal item of some sort, the odds of his success would be increased. The trick was getting close enough without anyone in the house seeing him. Driving up to the barn or one of the other outbuildings wouldn't raise any suspicions. Because there were other ranch hands already on the property, Jorge figured whoever was in the house with his boss wasn't worried about interference from the hired help.

Jorge placed the binoculars on the seat beside him and cranked the ignition. His best gamble was to simply drive to the outbuilding nearest the main house. Sweat beaded his brow as Jorge made the long drive from the highway, past the main house, and parked by the building that used to house an outdoor kitchen and now had become a repository for various yard and garden implements. Anyone familiar with the ranch would question why Jorge was going inside what was basically an unused garden shed. Jorge hoped the devil wouldn't know the difference.

Jorge had angled the driver's side of his truck away from the main house. Quickly, he unloaded the box containing the items he would need to invoke the spirits. He had charged the quartz tiger's eye early that morning with his own energy when the sun's first rays hit the earth. The stone, which appeared to emit a shimmering glow, lay nestled on a soft cloth. A small pouch of sea salt, a pen and paper, matches, and a crucifix completed the container's contents. The power of the spell would come from the words Jorge would utter. A strong *brujo* or *curandero* had no need of props such as those he had brought with him, but Jorge was not as strong as Miguel or his *abuela*. And he was untested.

Jorge shouldered the box of magical items and sauntered toward the rear of the main house. If anyone noticed his approach, Jorge hoped his appearance would seem nonthreatening—just another ranch hand doing menial work. A few minutes later, relief washed over Jorge when he had successfully navigated the short distance. Darting behind a stack of firewood, Jorge placed the box on the ground. *Now for the more dangerous part.* Jorge reminded himself to stay alert as he sprinted toward the black van, rolling underneath the vehicle to emerge on the side not readily visible from the house.

"Protect yourself," Jorge heard his *abuela* whisper. Acknowledging his grandmother's warning, Jorge stopped to center himself. Jorge closed his eyes and forced his heart to slow by taking several deep and slow breaths. When he felt calm, Jorge intoned, "Oh, spirits of light, protectors of the innocent, wielders of justice, hear my call." Opening his inner eye, Jorge saw those he had implored for protection. Great beings of light, appearing as ancient soldiers, formed a circle around Jorge. Facing away from him, the beings held aloft flaming swords. "Now, protect *them*," his *abuela*'s soft voice ordered.

Jorge reached for the handle of the passenger door. Pushing against the handle, Jorge felt the latch depress and release. Carefully, Jorge slowly opened the door just enough to peer inside. The smell of stale cigarettes assaulted Jorge's nose. As his attention drew to the source of the offending odor, Jorge spied an open and overflowing ashtray on the vehicle's lower dashboard. *Perfect.* Jorge smiled as he retrieved a handful of smoked butts, quietly closed the car door, and crawled back to his hiding place behind the woodpile.

Taking the pouch of salt, Jorge poured out the grainy substance, forming a large circle around him and the other items that he had removed from the box. "The breath of life and the light of my mind, create an enchantment of protection. The air I breathe is purified as I surround myself with an orb of gold," Jorge recited as he walked the circle. "I am purified and separated from all evil. This space is sacred and protected." Jorge examined the circle of salt. There were no breaks. Satisfied, Jorge placed himself in the center of the protected circle. There, he laid out the cigarette butts that had touched the devil's lips. Next to them, he laid the silver crucifix. "Son of all creation, send your protection."

The next step was important and dangerous. The protection circle had called upon Jorge's *curandero* magic, white magic. The magic that Jorge intended to invoke for the banishment spell was *brujo* magic, dark magic, that would call to the devil but that might also destroy Jorge and those he was trying to protect. Miguel Santera had been quite specific. "Whatever you write upon the paper I am sending to you will be more powerful than you can imagine. This paper is deeply imbued with *brujo* magic. The words of the banishment spell must be written with focused and specific intent. You must write, speak the spell, and then burn the paper." Jorge replayed the *brujo* magician's words in his mind. "Be careful what you ask. Even if you are able to call in the dark magic—and frankly, I doubt that you have that ability—you will not be able to direct it. Dark magic finds its own way, its own solution. All you can do is summon the forces of darkness."

Dismissing the trepidation that plucked at his gut, Jorge picked up the paper containing the powerful magic. Jorge considered his words carefully, remembering Miguel's warning. Intent was important.

First and foremost was his intention to protect Sean McIntosh and anyone else the devil had taken captive inside the ranch house. Jorge would try to banish the evil spirit but failing that, incapacitate the devil enough for Jorge to initiate a rescue.

Jorge grasped the tiger's eye in his left hand and uttered an incantation, invoking the power of the number three in his third petition for protection. Then, unclasping the gold chain, Jorge removed the amulet and placed it on the *brujo* paper that lay before him on the rocky ground. He had done all he could to protect himself. Picking up the pen, Jorge began to write. *Spirit to spirit, I invoke the magic of the* brujos, *the power gifted to me by my ancestors, the power to command the darkness and all of its minions. I, Jorge Roberto Jesus Velasquez, wielder of* brujo *magic, protected by the magic of the* curandero, *command you, spirits of the underworld, to do my bidding.* Jorge focused every fiber of his being on the paper before him, rejecting all self-doubt. *Banish the evil that inhabits the flesh inside this house. Remove the demon, and return him to hell. So do I command.*

With shaking hands, Jorge reached for the matchbook. All that remained was to burn the paper. The *brujo* magic would be released, and soon Jorge would know whether he had been strong enough to wield the power his *abuela* had assured him was his. Jorge cupped his hands to strike the match, but the sound of a rapidly approaching vehicle caught his attention. Glancing toward the driveway, Jorge recognized the large Ford truck barreling toward the ranch house. What was Sean's cousin doing here? Who was that with him? If he broke the circle to warn them...

CHAPTER FORTY

"If they haven't answered the door by now, they aren't going to," Allison remarked. "Nobody's here, Frank. Quit ringing that bell."

"That's Sean's Land Rover." Frank pointed to the gray over-the-road vehicle. "And someone else is here, too. There's a new model van parked over there at the side of the house."

"Frank, if Sean was here, he'd have answered the door by now." Allison was ready to head back to Fort Charles. "You've about beaten that door to pieces on top of ringing the bell twenty times."

"Have not," Frank huffed. "I'm telling you, something ain't right. Maria Sanchez isn't at her store, probably been gone for a couple of days given that note. Sean's car is here, but no one is answering the door. And who in the hell owns that black van over there? Looks like an FBI car, what with those blacked-out windows and all." Frank returned to pounding on the front door. "I know you're in there, Sean. I'm not leaving. Open the damn door."

To Allison's and Frank's surprise, the door opened two or three inches, constrained by a safety chain that obscured the identity of the person inside the house. "Senor McIntosh is not receiving guests today," a woman's voice informed the pair.

"I'm not a freakin' guest," Frank boomed. "I'm Sean's cousin, Frank Martin. Now, open this door."

"I am sorry, senor, but I have my orders," the woman replied.

"Did Mr. McIntosh give you those orders?" Allison leaned toward the narrow opening.

"No." Allison heard the sob behind the woman's answer. "It is best if you leave now."

"Wait." Allison tried to block the closing of the door with her foot. "Who are you?"

"Help us." The reply was so faint that Allison was unsure she had heard actual words. Before she could react, the front door of the ranch house slammed shut.

Allison motioned for Frank to follow her lead. "Well, I guess that answers that." Allison spoke louder than necessary. "Apparently, your cousin doesn't want any company. You ready to head back to Fort Charles?"

Frank wasn't sure what was going on, but whatever it was, it was clear that Allison was playing a part for someone other than him. "Yeah, maybe I pissed him off last time I visited," Frank replied hoping he was giving the right response. "I'm ready to head home if you are."

Walking away from the ranch house with their backs to anyone watching them from inside, Allison whispered, "She asked for help. You're right, Frank. Something's going on."

"Get in the truck like normal," Frank instructed. "We'll drive off the property and then circle back. There's a dirt farm road a couple of miles down the highway that comes in behind the cattle barn. Sean showed me last time I was down. We'll reconnoiter from there."

"Hurry, Frank." Allison was worried. "I've got a bad feeling about this."

Frank passed the turnoff twice before he finally found the dirt track. "Shit," he cursed as he dropped the truck's gear to four-wheel drive and accelerated down the goat path that doubled as an access road. "Hang on, Allison. It's going to be a rough ride."

Allison grabbed the sissy bar above the passenger side window. "Frank, I think we need to call the local sheriff. There's no telling what we're walking into."

Frank's head made contact with the cab's metal roof. "Damn," he exclaimed, not slowing down. "That hurt." Frank wrestled with the truck's steering wheel. "This road is worse than I remembered."

"Frank," Allison barked, "did you hear what I said? We need to call local law enforcement. This deal has bad news written all over it."

"Go ahead." Frank gave Allison a sharp look. "But I'm not waiting for backup."

"Agree," Allison replied, "but we're going to be careful. We have no idea what's going on, if this is a hostage situation, or how many people are in that house, armed or otherwise."

"This is as close as I can get without the truck being seen or heard," Frank informed Allison. "Make your call, then we're gonna find out what's really going on up there."

Allison dialed 911. After identifying herself and giving Frank's name, Allison quickly and succinctly gave the operator their location, the possible hostage scenario, and the request for immediate law enforcement response. Hoping her next statement would prove to be an exaggeration, Allison ended the call by telling the operator, "This is a matter of life and death."

"I've got a couple of extra clips that'll fit your GLOCK." Frank handed the magazines to Allison. "Good thing you brought your weapon."

"Never leave home without it anymore," Allison reminded Frank.

Frank shrugged a shoulder holster over his girth, pocketed extra clips for his own gun, then reached behind the driver's seat to retrieve a shotgun. "Never know when I might need this baby," Frank explained. "Let's go."

A thought crossed Allison's mind. "Two seconds, Frank," she interjected, holding up her hand. Grabbing her phone, Allison punched in a text. He might be four hours away by car, but he was right next door electronically. A call from Sheriff Trowbridge to his counterpart in Gilchrist County would be more effective that her call to the 911 operator. Satisfied that she had called in all the backup she could, Allison exited the truck and followed Frank.

CHAPTER FORTY-ONE

"Who was that?" Plato McCall thrust his angry face next to Maria Sanchez's terrified one. "Did he see you?"

"No, senor." Maria trembled. "He said he was Senor McIntosh's cousin. I have never seen him before."

Plato McCall grabbed Maria's arm, pulling her harshly down the short hallway into the paneled office where he had left Sean McIntosh bound and gagged. "Sit down," he growled, shoving Maria against the side of a small, upholstered chair. "And shut up." McCall paced the room. The unexpected disturbance had rattled him. "What's the deal with your cousin?"

Plato pulled the gag from Sean's mouth, demanding an answer.

"He's just my cousin." Sean's shrugged his shoulders. "Frank lives up in Fort Charles, Alabama."

"That's a long ways from here," McCall replied. "What's he doing down here?"

"Beats me." Sean hoped his answer would convince his captor. If Frank was at the ranch, he was most certainly there on business—Blue Scarlet business. "We hadn't seen each other since we were wee uns till a few months ago. I invited him to come for a visit any time he wanted," Sean fibbed. "Guess he took me up on the invitation."

Suspicion coated Plato's face. Nobody stopped by "just to visit." Plato pulled aside the closed window shade and peered out. Sean's cousin's truck was gone, but who did that beat-up pickup belong to, the one parked by the shed behind the house? It hadn't been there an hour ago when he last checked. "What's that building back there?" he demanded of Sean. "And who does that white single-cab truck belong to?"

Sean considered Plato's question. There shouldn't be anyone parked that close to the house. If the truck belonged to whom he thought it did, Jorge could be in great danger. His answer would be important. "That's just an old shed I use to store crap. Can't see the use of throwing something out that might prove useful down the road."

"And the truck?" Plato asked, still peering through the side of the opened window shade. "Who owns that truck?"

"How the hell do I know?" Sean feigned irritated indifference. "Probably one of the spics working for me. I don't pay attention to what some Mexican laborer drives. If it's old and beat up, it probably belongs to one of the workers."

Plato debated his next course of action. He wasn't worried about Sean's ranch employees. Half of them were probably illegal; they wouldn't risk getting sent back across the border just to help some gringo. Sean's cousin was another matter. "Who was that with your cousin?" Plato glanced at Sean and then back to Maria. "I thought I heard a woman's voice."

"What did she look like, Maria?" Sean asked. Hearing Maria's description of Frank's companion caused Sean an involuntary startle. If Allison Parker was with Frank, the visit had significance. And if Sean knew anything about his cousin, he hoped he knew what Frank was doing now. Sean's ability to assure Plato McCall that Frank was not a threat could mean the difference between life and death, not just for him but for everyone else. "Oh, I bet that's Frank's fiancée. He told me he was getting married." Sean was amazed at how easily he could lie. "That's probably why he came down—wanted to surprise me and introduce the gal he plans on marrying."

"Hmm." Plato considered Sean's explanation. Could be true, but why take a chance? "Too bad you won't be around for the wedding." Plato's smile belied the deadly prediction. Turning away from the window, Plato reached for the coiled rope that lay nearby. "Nor you." Plato struck Maria with a fisted hand, knocking her unconscious.

"Leave her alone!" Sean yelled. "You fucking son of a bitch, leave her alone!"

Satisfied that Maria's bindings were secure, Plato turned his attention to Sean. "That was my plan— my original plan. You're the one I want, not that piece of trash," Plato explained. "But when I realized what she meant to you, that made my revenge all the sweeter."

Keep him talking. Buying time was Sean's only weapon. "I don't know what you think there is between Maria and me, but it's not what you think."

"Oh, she's just a good lay, is that it?" Plato McCall laughed. "Good try, McIntosh, but I don't buy it for a minute. She's the mother of your kid, isn't she?"

"No, she's not," Sean retorted. "If the kid were mine, do you think I'd have shut her away with a bunch of nuns?"

Plato ignored Sean's denial. The earlier intrusion still bothered him. Best to finish this and make his escape. Plato reached into the large bag he had stowed near the doorway, withdrawing a can of gasoline. Slowly and methodically, he poured the acrid liquid around the room. "It took me a while to decide on the proper punishment for you." Plato spread the fuel around the chair where Sean was tied. "Just shooting you seemed so pedestrian." Seeing Sean's puzzled look, Plato replied. "Oh, I'd planned to shoot you when you brought me the money for that freakin' horse, but someone beat me to it. Too bad for you that you survived. Death by burning is much worse and much, much slower."

Sean pushed the visual from his mind, concentrating on what he had just learned. Plato didn't know Sean had sent Frank to the money drop. Could he use that to his advantage? Stall for more time? It was worth a try. "That wasn't me."

Plato stopped pouring. "What do you mean?"

"I didn't go to the drop. Whoever got there before you, they shot a PI I had hired." Sean worked the ropes that held his hands, hoping Plato would not see his covert movements. "There's nothing to tie you to Blue Scarlet. No one's looking for you." Sean felt the rope loosen. "Walk out now, and I promise I won't tell the cops anything."

"And why would I do that?" Plato questioned.

"Because I still have the money" Sean pulled against his bindings. All he needed was a minute or two longer. "Untraceable and in small bills, just like you wanted."

"I don't need your money." Plato tossed the empty gasoline container in the corner. "Just your death." Plato McCall held up a silver cigarette lighter, flicked open the shiny top, and clicked the igniter.

CHAPTER FORTY-TWO

Sean's cousin had left, and with his exit, Jorge's only hope for a physical intervention. The *brujo's* instructions had been clear. Draw the circle, recite the words of the spell, and then light the paper on which he had written the enchantment. But Jorge had hesitated, waiting to see what Sean's cousin would do. Too much time had passed. *Should I start again?* Jorge wished he knew the answer. He would have only one shot at success. Delaying to start over might be too late. *Think*, he commanded himself. *And ask for guidance.*

Jorge sat cross-legged in the center of the protected circle. Opening his hands palm up and laying them on his thighs, Jorge closed his eyes and turned inward. Slowly, as he had been taught so many years before, Jorge watched his chakras glow with the rainbow lights of their own energy. Beginning with the red of his root chakra, Jorge moved his conscious mind to his crown, to the indigo light, and propelling himself higher, into the circle of gold above his physical body. There, he rested, waiting.

A figure formed in the distance. Shadowy, indistinct but clearly feminine—not in ways that could be seen but known nevertheless. "*Abuela?*" Jorge silently questioned. "*The circle is unbroken.*" Images rather than words came to Jorge, yet he understood their meaning. "*The magic is strong. It is yours to command.*" Jorge felt his body become warm, then hot, as the powerful energy flowing from the figure before him began to course through his veins, violently breaking the connection to the greater reality. Opening his eyes, Jorge reached for the tiger's eye and began to chant.

"Look, Frank. The window on the side of the house, near the front." Allison nudged the PI. "Someone moved the shade aside. Just for a few seconds."

"If Sean and Maria are being held against their will, it makes sense the perp would have them in the same room, incapacitated, where he could keep an eye on them." Frank motioned for Allison to follow him. "We need to get closer."

Allison glanced at her watch. "I don't know how far out the sheriff's office is from the ranch. Couldn't be far. Bell isn't that big. I think we ought to wait. Help ought to be here any minute."

"If Jim had waited for backup with Jefferson Boudreaux, you'd be dead now," Frank reminded Allison. "We can't take that risk."

Nodding, Allison hurried behind Frank as the pair ran as fast as a crouched position would allow. Plastering themselves against the side of the ranch house and next to the window where Allison had seen movement, the two took a moment to catch their breath. "We need to get inside the house," Frank observed. "I'm going to try the back. You stay here."

Allison grabbed Frank's collar, yanking the large man's face close to hers. "Frank Martin," she hissed, "you can't go in alone." Allison placed her hand over Frank's mouth, silencing his objection. "Either we go in together or we both stay out here. Staying out here doesn't help Sean."

"Keep behind me," Frank ordered. "Way back. If this goes sideways, one of us needs to be able to escape."

Quickly, the pair moved to the back of the ranch house and climbed the short trio of steps to the enclosed back porch. "Shh," Allison cautioned as the screened porch door gave a squeak. "Quiet."

"I'm being as quiet as I can," Frank grumbled. "I just hope the back door is unlocked."

Allison waited until Frank was positioned by the kitchen door. Taking care to close the screen door as silently as possible, Allison took up her position to Frank's immediate left. 'On your order," she whispered. "I've got your six."

"Banish the evil that inhabits the flesh inside this house. Remove the demon, and return him to hell. So do I command." Jorge spit the words, imbuing them with the energy that still coursed through his body. Holding the paper aloft, Jorge touched it with the match he struck. "So do I command," he repeated. "I, Jorge Roberto Jesus Velasquez, wielder of *brujo* magic, protected by the light of *curandero*."

Jorge's ears popped painfully as the air pressure around him suddenly dropped. Although he saw nothing moving outside the circle, Jorge felt a cold wind moving violently over his body. The *brujo* paper that Jorge had ignited floated before him, held invisibly by the wind, yet undamaged by it. Suddenly, a brilliant flash exploded within the circle. Jorge cried out, throwing his arms across his face to shield his eyes.

"For God's sake, don't do this," Sean McIntosh pleaded. "Kill me, but spare Maria and the child." Almost. He almost had his hands freed.

"What would be the fun in that?" Plato McCall asked. With a laugh, he threw the flaming lighter to the floor.

A blood curdling shriek assaulted Frank and Allison. "Now!" Frank shouted, pushing open the kitchen door and running toward the horrific screaming. Adrenaline fueled Allison, giving her the edge on Frank's labored attempt at speed. Passing the PI, Allison ran toward the front of the ranch house, fighting the urge to vomit as the smell of burning flesh rose to meet her advance.

The shrieking had stopped, replaced by a man's voice calling for help. Pointing her GLOCK with both hands, Allison edged quickly around the open doorway. In the corner, a crumpled figure lay twisted, flames consuming the form, licking and making crackling sounds. The sight was more than Allison could handle. Abruptly, she bent over and emptied the contents of her stomach.

"Sean, are you all right?" Frank Martin slammed past Allison, hurrying to assist his cousin who was holding a bleeding woman in his arms. "We've got to get out of here. The house could go at any moment."

Sean McIntosh remained unresponsive to Frank's urging. Placing her arms around Sean McIntosh, Allison urged, "Sean, Sean, you have to help us."

A soft moan escaped the woman's lips, rousing Sean from his trance. "Maria," he whispered, coming to his senses. "Get her out," he ordered. "I've got to find Isabella."

The smell of gasoline had become overwhelming. The fumes were beginning to burn Allison's eyes. "Oh my God," she exclaimed. "There's gasoline everywhere. The carpet is soaked." Frantically, Allison urged her companions to flee. "Frank, I'll take Sean with me, look for this Isabella person. You get Maria outside." Turning to Sean, Allison asked for confirmation. "This is Maria Sanchez, isn't it?"

Frank hoisted Maria onto his shoulder using a fireman's carry. "Hurry, Allison," he called as headed out of the house.

"Yes," Sean replied to Allison's question. "Isabella is her daughter. She's in the back bedroom, at the other end of the house." Without further comment, Sean turned and ran down a narrow hallway to his right.

Allison hurried to keep up. Behind her, she could feel heat from the expanding conflagration. "The fire's spreading," Allison warned. "We don't have much time."

"In here." Sean stopped at the next door and turned the knob. "Locked." Sean glared. "That monster locked her in." Stepping back, Sean ran at the door, attacking the obstruction with his body. Nothing. The door remained closed.

"Move." Allison pushed Sean aside. Leveling her aim, Allison fired directly into the door's locking mechanism. "Try it now."

With one swift kick, the door sprang open. On the narrow bed lay a small child whose frightened eyes told Allison all she needed to know. "It's OK, baby," Allison crooned as she gathered the little girl to her chest. "We've got you."

Sean, Allison, and Isabella had barely cleared the house when a huge explosion shook the ground. "Where're Frank and Maria?" Sean cried.

"Here, over here." Allison and Sean turned to the sound of Frank's voice. A man Allison remembered as one of Sean's ranch hands was tending to Maria Sanchez. Frank was standing guard, gun at the ready. "Jorge saw me carrying Maria. He's helping her."

Allison recognized the name. Jorge Velasquez was the man who had told Frank about Maria Sanchez. Allison wondered what Jorge's role was in all that had just transpired. It seemed a bit too fortuitous that Jorge had appeared at just the right time to render assistance. The rest of the ranch hands were only now running toward the house, presumably in response to the fiery explosion that had just occurred.

"My baby." Maria reached out her arms to claim her child.

"Mama." The little girl hid her face in her mother's breast and began to cry.

The sound of a siren caught Allison's attention. "Here comes our backup," she observed wryly. "Good thing we made do without them." Two county squad cars, dust roiling up from their wheels as they careened off the drive and across the lawn toward the huddled group, blared their arrival.

"Reckon by now they've called the fire department," Frank remarked. "Although by the looks of your house, Sean, I think it's a total loss." Leaving the group, Frank walked over to meet the deputies who were pouring out of the two cars. He had a lot of explaining to do.

"What happened in there, Sean?" Allison wanted to know. "Whose body was that?"

Sean McIntosh leaned over to kiss Maria Sanchez's head before standing to address the question his rescuer had posed. "His name was Plato McCall. Years ago, I happened on him while he was trying to kidnap his sister. My involvement and subsequent testimony at his trial sent him to prison. He told me he was getting his revenge." Sean proceeded to explain about McCall stealing Blue Scarlet, leaving out a few pertinent details.

"And Maria?" Allison asked. "What about her?"

"Collateral damage." Sean had no intention of implicating Maria. "Wrong place at the wrong time."

Allison brushed a stray lock of hair from her face. Her hands and clothes smelled like gas and smoke. "There's something else, too, Sean. That room was soaked in gasoline. Every bit of it, yet the only thing burning when Frank and I got to you was the body."

Sean nodded but didn't answer.

"How did that happen, Sean? How did that man burn to a crisp in just a few minutes, and the rest of the room remain untouched? Or at least untouched until we got you, Maria, and Isabella out?"

Sean McIntosh shook his head. "As long as I live, I'll never be rid of what I saw in there," Sean began. "I thought we were dead. McCall poured a can of gasoline all over the carpet and around me and Maria. When he threw the lit cigarette lighter on the floor, I was praying for a quick end." Sean looked at his raw, bleeding wrists. "I had just gotten my hands free. I hoped maybe I could get to Maria first, get her out. And then it happened."

"What happened?" Allison pushed.

"Never seen anything like it." Sean blanched as the horrific memory replayed in his mind. "Don't know how it was possible given all that gasoline in the carpet. When the lighter hit the rug, a wall of flame arose around McCall, like it was embracing him, refusing to let him go. Nothing else burned. Nothing except him."

Allison stood in stunned silence. Neither she nor Sean saw the satisfied smile that crossed Jorge's face.

CHAPTER FORTY-THREE

A week had passed since Sean McIntosh's house had burned to the ground. The Gilchrist County medical examiner had positively identified the charred human remains using dental records. No doubt about it, the dead man was, indeed, who he had claimed to be in life. When the Gilchrist County sheriff reached out to Plato McCall's next of kin, he was quickly rebuffed with a "He's in hell where he ought to be. Dump his remains. We don't want him."

Allison knew from talking with Frank Martin a few days after their return to Fort Charles that Frank was trying to talk his cousin into selling the ranch in Bell and moving closer to Fort Charles. "I didn't realize how much having family meant to me until I almost lost Sean," Frank had explained to Allison. "There's plenty of good land up here and no bad memories." Allison thought Frank's idea was a good one. Whether Sean McIntosh would agree remained to be seen. For Frank's sake, Allison hoped his cousin said yes.

Today, Allison was headed to Toby Trowbridge's office. The Calhoun County sheriff had invited—invited being a polite expression—Allison and Frank for a detailed debriefing. Allison had suggested that Sean McIntosh be present as well. The information Sean had shared with her after the house explosion had convinced Allison that there was potentially more to the theft of Blue Scarlet than Toby's office had originally surmised. With Plato McCall dead, the additional information might not have any value, but Allison felt Toby ought to be the one to make that decision.

The parking lot for the Calhoun County Sheriff's Office and county jail was already full when Allison pulled in at 8:30 a.m. for the meeting. *Must be something interesting going on at the courthouse.* Allison picked her brain, trying to remember if Jim had mentioned any unusual cases on today's docket. When nothing came to mind, Allison dismissed the mental question. She had more on her mind than wondering what was going on in her husband's courtroom. If it had been anything of significance, Jim would have mentioned it to her at breakfast. Spying a strip of asphalt at the back of the lot, Allison slid her car into the last remaining spot.

"Mornin', Ms. Parker." A young deputy waved Allison around the building's metal detectors. "Sheriff said to send you right in."

"Thanks, Tom." Allison smiled. "Stay safe today."

"Can't see that being hard to do." The deputy laughed. "Nothing much ever happens around here."

Forgoing a reply, Allison hurried down the main hallway to the anteroom adjacent to the sheriff's private office. Beth Robinson, the sheriff's octogenarian secretary and gatekeeper, waved a greeting. "Frank Martin called. Said he'd be a few minutes late. You ask me, that's because he's stopping to stuff his face at the doughnut shop." Allison grinned. Whatever Beth Robinson thought came directly out of her mouth. "He thinks he can hide the evidence"—Beth sniffed—"but I can smell sugar a mile away."

"Well," Allison allowed, "Frank does have a weakness for sweets."

"I'm going to give that boy a piece of my mind," Beth huffed. "I heard tell that doctor up in Birmingham told Frank to lose weight if he didn't want to die." Angrily, Beth shuffled an already-perfectly stacked pile of papers on her desk. "So long as I live,

I won't never understand how men folk can be so stupid."

"You go, girl." Allison laughed. "Tell Frank exactly what you think when he gets here." *I can't wait to hear what Frank has to say to that.* Allison was still laughing when she walked into Toby's office.

"She's on a rampage today," Allison remarked to the head of Calhoun County law enforcement.

Sheriff Trowbridge swiveled his desk chair to face Allison and motioned for her to take a seat. "Beth only gets like this about the people she loves."

"I know." Allison crossed her legs and leaned back in the one comfortable chair in the sheriff's office. "And she called him 'boy,' too. That's hilarious."

Toby handed Allison a cup of coffee, adding "It's fresh" in response to her raised eyebrows. "Frank is a boy as far as Beth is concerned. She's well old enough to be his mother and in some circles, his grandmother."

Allison had just finished telling Toby about Charlotte's next riding competition when a loud commotion announced Frank's arrival and Beth's tongue lashing. Beth's "You better listen to me, young man" threat followed a frantic Frank Martin into the sheriff's office space.

"Good Lord Almighty, Toby," Frank bellowed. "That woman's not right in the head." The responding laughter from Allison and the sheriff irked Frank further. "Stop laughing, y'all. It's not funny."

"Oh, but it is Frankie, me boy," Sean McIntosh followed his cousin into the office. "That old granny has your number, plain and simple."

By the time Allison had regained her composure and wiped the tears from her face, Frank and Sean had settled into the office's two remaining chairs in response to the sheriff's request that they "cut the crap and get down to business."

Sean McIntosh started. "You all know the first part. My horse Blue Scarlet was stolen, and I hired Frank to look into the theft." Sean looked at his cousin. "You still don't remember any of that, do you?"

Frank shook his head. "Can't remember a darn thing between the day before I got shot till I woke up two weeks later in the hospital."

Sean paused to light a pipe he had pulled from his jacket pocket. "Well, when I told Frank about the ransom demand, he insisted he go in my stead." Sean tapped the pipe's bowl against the palm of his hand, discarding the smoked tobacco into a nearby waste can. "I thought it was a bad idea and told him so. And I was right." Sean and Frank traded turns talking, Frank describing his efforts in the investigation after he was discharged from the hospital, while Sean interrupted a few times to comment.

"Wait a minute." Allison realized what had been bugging her about the meeting place for the ransom drop. "Maybe I've missed something, but why was the ransom drop set for the old Anderson place? Why not in Bell or someplace closer than here."

"Frank's idea," Sean replied. "I convinced the horsenapper—who we now know was Plato McCall—that I owned the Anderson property and that it was a safer place for the meet."

"That's weak," Toby argued. "A drop four hours away from where you live? I can't believe McCall fell for it."

"Criminals are stupid," Frank allowed with a snort. "They fall for all sorts of shit. That's why they get caught."

Sean finished tamping down the fresh tobacco he had placed in his pipe. "Doesn't really matter. McCall told me he was there that night and had planned to kill me, but someone else had gotten there ahead of him." The sweet smell of tobacco filled the room. "He thought I was the one who had been shot that night."

"Which brings us to the other reason I called this meeting," Sheriff Trowbridge interjected. "We still don't know who shot Frank. Whoever that was, I want to know who it is, and why Frank was targeted. After listening to Mr. McIntosh, and based on what we know about Plato McCall's motives, we're no closer now to finding Frank's attacker than we were the night he got shot."

"Actually, that's not exactly true," Frank contradicted the sheriff.

"You know something I don't?" Toby asked.

A grim smile crossed Frank's face. "It never made sense to me that the horsenapper would shoot me and leave the ransom money I had with me." Frank shifted his weight, trying to find a comfortable position in the undersize, wood chair. "Uh, let me correct that. I can see the horsenapper killing me if he thought I was Sean, but he wouldn't have left the money."

Allison considered Frank's remarks. "Makes sense, but who else would have been there that night? Did anyone else know about the drop?"

"Think outside the box," Frank suggested. "What if my shooting had nothing to do with the ransom?"

"I know you've pissed off a lot of people over the years," Toby interjected, "but who would want to kill you?"

Reaching into his jacket pocket, Frank retrieved his iPhone. "I made a list." Frank punched the notes icon. "Went over every open case I had at the time I was shot, even looked at the nasty ones from the last twelve months. I came up with one possible suspect, someone who would have a reason to really hate me."

Sean laid his still-warm pipe on the sheriff's desk, disregarding Toby's disapproving stare. "Well, don't keep us in suspense. Who is it?"

"Pierre Chastain."

"Who the hell is Pierre Chastain?" Sean asked.

"A local schoolteacher who lost his job and probably his teaching career," Toby explained. "He was implicated in a big sex scandal here that resulted in a nasty divorce trial."

"Frank ended up being a key witness for the wronged spouse," Allison addressed her remarks to Sean. "Jim told me after the trial was over that Frank's testimony was the most damaging evidence against Evelyn Goodpasture."

"Wait a minute." Sean waved his hands in a time-out signal. "Who is Jim? What did you say that would make this Pierre guy want to kill you? Was he the one getting the divorce?"

"The Goodpasture divorce was a sordid affair." Frank summarized his involvement in the court case for his cousin. "Pierre Chastain lost his job and probably his livelihood, and Mavis Johnson killed herself." Frank shook his head. "Mavis's suicide was something none of us expected."

"Jim is my husband," Allison added. "He's the judge who tried the case."

"It's a long shot, but if Plato McCall was telling the truth, Frank's shooter is still out there," Toby stated. "I'll put out an APB on Chastain, see if law enforcement can track him down. Once we find him, I'll bring him in for questioning."

A few minutes later, the group had disbanded with Toby assuring everyone he'd be in touch as soon as he had a location on Pierre Chastain. Allison, Sean, and Frank exited the sheriff's office together and headed toward the parking lot.

"I've never seen this lot so packed," Allison commented to the two men.

"I have an idea why," Frank replied. "Taylor Kitchens left a message for me on the office phone last night. Evelyn Goodpasture's lawyer has filed a motion for a new trial. It's being argued today. Taylor thought I might want to attend the hearing." Frank motioned to the overflow of cars lining the street in front of the courthouse. "By the look of things, most of Fort Charles is here as well."

All judges set aside a day or half day each week for hearing motions—motions for a new trial, motions to compel discovery, with motions for a continuance being the most common. Many judges designated Fridays as motion days for reasons unknown other than maybe as a vehicle for having a shorter workday at the beginning of the weekend. Allison's husband had bucked the unspoken traditional motion day, choosing instead Monday as motion day in his courtroom. "That would explain why Jim didn't mention anything to me this morning," Allison replied. "He usually has no idea what motions have been put on the Monday docket until he arrives at the courthouse."

"I haven't heard anything overly salacious in a while." Sean McIntosh chuckled. "Want to join me for a gander, Frankie boy? This might be quite entertaining."

Frank considered the offer. He didn't have any appointments until later in the day. "Why not?" he replied. "Want to come along, Allison?"

The facts of the Goodpasture case made Allison sad. The way Fort Charles's society had treated Evelyn Goodpasture had made her even sadder. Cases like this one took a toll on everyone—the parties, the attorneys, and especially the judge when the law required a decision that was going to have a particularly adverse effect on the losing party, just like had happened to Evelyn Goodpasture. "I'll walk over with y'all, see where the case is on the motion docket." Allison glanced at the calendar app on her phone. "I've got an eleven o'clock, so I can't stay very long."

CHAPTER FORTY-FOUR

Judge Jim Kaufman's courtroom was full of spectators. Surveying the crowd from the vantage point of the bench, Jim pounded his gavel for quiet. "I know why most of you are here today," he began, "and while this courtroom is open to the public, I will not tolerate inappropriate behavior, commentary, or rowdiness." Jim paused to let his words sink in. "This is the only warning you will get. I know most of you, and believe me when I tell you none of you want to spend time in jail for contempt of court."

Allison, Frank, and Sean slipped into the courtroom in time to hear the judge's final admonition. Leaning toward Sean, Allison whispered, "He means it, too. Jim doesn't put up with any nonsense in his courtroom."

"Call the docket," Jim instructed his courtroom administrator, Nancy Curtis. Seated to the judge's left where normally a witness would sit during trial, Nancy began calling the names of the various cases that had been scheduled on the day's docket. "*Commerce People's Bank v. Johnson; National Paper v. Weems; Fairchild v. Smith.*" Various lawyers rose to acknowledge their presence and readiness in response to their cases being called. When Nancy had finished, lawyers for fifteen cases had replied in the affirmative, and two had asked for continuances to the next available motion day.

"Jim hears the simple motions first," Allison explained to Sean McIntosh. "Based on what I've heard so far, the Goodpasture case will be near the end."

"Is the Goodpasture woman here?" Sean was curious. After what he had heard in the sheriff's office, Sean wanted to see what the woman with all the lovers looked like.

Allison and Frank perused the room. "Don't see her," Frank remarked.

"The parties don't usually attend motion hearings," Allison explained to Sean. "These are legal arguments. Generally no live testimony is given, so there's no reason for anyone other than the lawyers to be here."

A soft vibration in her jacket pocket caught Allison's attention. "Looks like my eleven o'clock has canceled," she informed her companions. "Donna just sent me a text. I'll hang out with y'all and see if Jim can grab lunch with us. I know he'd like to meet you, Sean."

The remainder of the morning passed quickly. Each case had its own distinct flavor, and listening to the arguments put forth by the town's lawyers as well as lawyers from surrounding counties was both entertaining and enlightening. Allison's prediction had been right. All fourteen of the contested motions had been heard and ruled on by Jim Kaufman before the judge called the Goodpasture case forward. The courtroom had remained full as well.

"Mr. Lockridge, I believe this is your motion?" Judge Kaufman inquired.

"Yes, Your Honor." Mark Lockridge stood to respond formally. "I have a motion for a new trial."

"You may proceed." Jim nodded at Evelyn Goodpasture's lawyer.

Mark Lockridge put forth a surprisingly good argument given what he had to work with, offering up several creative legal theories for consideration by Judge Kaufman. *Interesting but unlikely to prove successful*, Allison thought as she listened to Lockridge explain to her husband why Evelyn Goodpasture deserved a new trial. By the time Taylor Kitchens had responded with his own arguments as to why the motion for a new trial should be denied, Allison felt confident that she knew what her husband's ruling would be.

"Thank you, counsel," Jim Kaufman acknowledged the lawyers' efforts. "As you are both aware, I generally rule on these motions from the bench. However, given the notoriety that has accompanied this case"—the judge stopped to glare at the courtroom's spectators—"I have decided to take the motion under advisement. I will issue a written opinion by the end of the week." Disregarding the disgruntled murmuring that had started inside the courtroom, Judge Kaufman struck the bench with his gavel, announced, "Court is adjourned," and left the room.

"Come on." Allison hurried toward the door that led directly to her husband's office. "We'll use Jim's private entrance."

Allison's knock was quickly answered. "Hey, Ms. Parker. Come on in. I saw you in the gallery and figured you'd be coming on back." Dickie Lee Bishop ushered Allison and her companions into the judge's chambers. "Hey, there, Mr. Martin," he added, giving a questioning look toward Sean McIntosh. "Judge Kaufman's in the restroom. He'll be out in just a few minutes." Dickie Lee's face reddened with the realization of what he'd just said.

"It's OK, Dickie Lee," Frank assured the embarrassed bailiff. "None of us gives a hoot about the judge's bathroom habits."

Jim's hearty "What is this? A party?" absolved Dickie Lee from the need to come up with an answer to Frank's comment. Meeting Allison's advance and unbothered by the small audience of men, Jim gave his wife a long kiss. "This is a nice surprise."

"We found ourselves with a free morning when we finished with Toby," Allison explained. "After Frank told me you were hearing the Goodpasture motion, the three of us decided to sit in." Motioning to Sean, Allison continued. "And I wanted to introduce you to Sean McIntosh, Frank's cousin."

Judge Kaufman offered Sean his hand. "Glad to meet you, McIntosh. I feel like I already know you given how much Allison has talked about you and the theft of your horse."

"Do you have time for lunch, Jim?" Allison asked. "The four of us could grab a bite before Sean heads back to Bell."

"Sounds like a plan." Jim smiled. "I don't get to have lunch with my beautiful wife very often. Let me tell Nancy I'll be out for about an hour."

The sounds of chimes emanating from the steeple bell at First Baptist Church had just started to announce the noon hour when the four exited the courthouse and descended the steps to Main Street.

"What a fabulous day," Allison remarked as a light breeze lifted her hair. "Let's see if we can get a patio table at the café. It's way too nice to eat inside." Allison turned toward her husband expecting him to voice his agreement to her suggestion. "Jim?" Allison was puzzled by the look on her husband's face.

"No!" Jim Kaufman yelled. The sound of gunfire erupted around her as Allison was violently pushed to the ground. Instinctively, she covered her head with her arms and rolled into a fetal position. The shooting seemed to go on forever. Later, Allison was told it was over in less than a minute.

"Lassie, are you hit?" Sean McIntosh gathered Allison in his arms.

Allison struggled to make sense of what had just happened. Someone had shot at her. Where was her husband? "Jim!" she cried out frantically. "Where's Jim?" Allison pushed against Sean. "Where is he?" Allison crawled toward a small crowd of people who had gathered on the steps a few feet away. She could see Frank's back. He was kneeling next to someone. *Please, God*, she prayed. *Please, not Jim, not my husband.*

God did not listen.

CHAPTER FORTY-FIVE

Jim Kaufman was buried with full military honors in the small graveyard next to the Episcopal church where his children, Charlotte and Mack, had been baptized as infants. So many people came to pay their respects that the priest had to open the parish hall to the overflow crowd where they could listen to the funeral service on the church's public address system that had recently been installed. Allison's brother, Rice, thin and weak from his latest round of chemo, had been given special permission by the prison warden at Kilby to attend his brother-in-law's funeral. "Judge Kaufman was one of the finest people I've ever known," Warden Zachary Stone told his inmate. "I'm going to the funeral. I'll take you with me."

Jake Cleveland, Wilson Mackey, and several other FBI agents from the Birmingham regional office also attended the funeral. "I'm proud to have known him," Jake told Allison. "Anything I can do for you, all you have to do is pick up the phone."

Ed Mitchum, whose daughter had died at the hands of a serial killer Allison had later apprehended, wept when he reached Allison during visitation before the funeral commenced. "I know how hard this is, Allison. First I lost Caroline and then Mindy. You and Jim were there for me both times." Ed tried unsuccessfully to gain control of his emotions. His lament, "I hate this," was barely audible as the man turned to find a seat inside the sanctuary.

David and Sarah Jackson never left Allison's side. Bereft of family, other than her brother, Rice, who was serving three life sentences in the penitentiary, Allison had clung to her partner and his wife for support over the days between Jim's murder and his funeral. Frank Martin, who everyone thought would have been a tower of strength for Allison, had barely been able to function. Instead, Frank had drowned himself in more than one bottle of Scotch whiskey, blaming himself for missing the clues that Frank believed could have saved his friend's life. It had taken an intervention by his cousin, Sean McIntosh, to sober up Frank for the funeral. Donna Pevey, grieving almost as much as Allison, had taken the distraught Parker-Kaufman children under her wing, trying to help ease the shock and confusion that their father's sudden death had wrought on the youngest members of the family.

Allison had asked Sheriff Trowbridge, Frank Martin, David Jackson, Dickie Lee Bishop, and two of Jim's longtime friends from his Marine days to serve as pallbearers. A hush fell over the congregants as the six men carrying Jim's flag-draped coffin entered the sanctuary, leading the processional to the front of the church. Father Bacon followed close behind, then Allison and her children. The sorrowful sound of weeping wafted over those gathered, reminding all of the sad reason for their attendance.

Although Allison and Jim had attended church sporadically, each followed a daily spiritual practice of prayer and meditation. When Allison and Jim had looked for a church home for their children, the rituals of the Episcopal Church had appealed to both of them. Over the years, Father Bacon had become a close family friend. Listening to the priest as he began his homily, Allison was grateful that Robert Bacon had known her husband as well as he had.

At the conclusion of Father Bacon's homily and closing prayer, the six pallbearers raised Jim's coffin onto their shoulders and led the family and congregants from the sanctuary to the graveyard behind the small stone church. There, the church's gravediggers had prepared the hallowed ground that would receive Jim Kaufman's mortal remains. When all had gathered, Father Bacon offered a brief prayer, then, gathering a handful of loose dirt from the upturned soil, the priest intoned, "In sure and certain hope of the resurrection to eternal life through our Lord Jesus Christ, we commend to Almighty God our brother James Kaufman, and we commit his body to the ground; earth to earth, ashes to ashes, dust to dust. The Lord bless him and keep him, the Lord make his face to shine upon him and be gracious unto him and give him peace. Amen."

Southern custom dictated a reception at the close of a burial service, generally at the home of the family who had just buried their loved one. A child of the Deep South and understanding the comfort that these postfuneral gatherings provided, Allison had made arrangements for a light repast at the farm following Jim's internment. By the time the last mourner had left her home, the adrenaline that had kept Allison running for the last few days was totally depleted.

"I'm staying here another night," Donna Pevey informed her boss. "I put Charlotte and Mack to bed two hours ago. You need to do the same. You won't be any good to your children if you don't get some rest."

"She's right." Sarah Jackson wrapped her arms around her friend. "Dr. Clarke left a sedative for you so you could sleep tonight." Sarah spoke quietly about inconsequential nonsense as she helped Allison undress and get ready for bed. "David and I will stay for a while longer. I'll be back first thing tomorrow." Sarah turned off the bedside lamp and closed the bedroom door behind her. Allison listened as her friend's footsteps faded down the hallway.

Life would go on—this Allison knew intellectually. But her heart was another matter. Laying her head on Jim's pillow, his scent still strong on the soft fabric, Allison submitted to the tears she had held at bay.

EPILOGUE

Allison laid the Christmas wreath on Jim's grave. "I love you, baby," she whispered. "Charlotte and Mack miss you terribly, and so do I, but I don't want you to worry about us." Allison traced the engraving on the granite marker with her finger. "I'm back at work, taking a few cases, just the ones that appeal to me. I'm grateful we've got the resources to give me that option. Charlotte has spent a lot of time out at the stables. Jeri Kennedy told me that riding Diamond Girl has been good therapy for our daughter. Losing you has been harder on Mack, but we're working on it. He's seeing Dr. Miller once a week. She says children have amazing resilience, and Mack will eventually come to terms with your death in a healthy way."

Allison gazed at the cloudless sky. In the distance, she could see the faint outline of the approaching cold front. Brushing leaves from the grass that covered her husband's resting place, Allison retrieved a small woolen blanket from her satchel, placed it over the mounded ground, and sat down. "Evelyn Goodpasture hanged herself last week. Toby had her on a suicide watch, waiting for her upcoming criminal trial, but she outsmarted him." Allison paused, thinking about all the pain that Evelyn had caused her. "I want to hate her, Jim, for taking you away from me, from our children, for leaving us alone. But I can't. All I can feel for that woman is pity. I hope you can understand."

Time passed. The warm sunshine was replaced by gray clouds and a cold north wind. Allison gathered her belongings reluctantly. "I forgive you, Jim, for losing your life." Allison's eyes filled with tears. "Evelyn confessed that I was the target. She told Toby she wanted to hurt you, to destroy your life like she believed you had destroyed hers. She was the one who shot Frank, too." Allison pressed her lips to the cold stone marker that bore her husband's name. "If you hadn't seen her and pushed me aside, I'd be the one lying here now. A Marine to the end." She sighed. "You did your duty, my love, and made the ultimate sacrifice."

A light snow had begun to fall by the time Allison reached her car. He husband had always kidded her about her love affair with the "white stuff." Turning her face upward, Allison accepted the snow's tickling kiss. "Thank you," she whispered. "I will love you forever."